Sins of the Flesh
Erotic Short Stories

By: Stacey Thomas

ISBN: 0615879608
ISBN-13: 978-0615879604

DEDICATION

To my mom, Robin Tucker, who always gives support, guidance and love.

ACKNOWLEDGMENTS

I would like to thank God for the gift of writing that he's given me and the knowledge of knowing that only he can judge. Thanks to my Editor and supporter Neiima Edwards, author of Chasing Forgiveness: Abortion a Life Sentence. A special thanks to Lisa Borders Muhammad for being an amazing marketer/promoter and Chris Ringo for the awesome book cover!

Thanks to: Laverne Wyatt constantly telling me that I had a gift for writing, and always giving support.

F.B. /L. Herring who always made it clear words were not enough; they needed to see an actual book in print. They are always motivating and supporting me.

Chris Ringo, I thank because at a very important time during this process he came through for me having patience and providing me with an awesome book cover.

Shenita Hill for her support and most importantly she leading me to a publisher when I started on this journey.

Ejae Thomas for believing in me and for his wise cracks about his mom's stories.

JW for believing in his mom even though he doesn't know what I write.

LaShunda Young for always believing in me as her sister. She never ceases to amaze me in speaking her mind. Fran Thomas for believing in me and supporting me, her older sister.

K.K. for always being honest, providing ideas and for always saying I can do it.

Leon Wyatt for his support and for believing in me.

To other supporters that I will only identify as IB, TJ, NB, TC, WW (Your Turn Now), MI, JJ, JW, A.R.

A BIG THANKS to my husband, who never tries to stop me when I constantly change careers!

To my Readers: Thanks so much for your support. I do hope that you receive enjoyment from my stories. If you have a dream, don't just dream, pursue it. It's never too late!

CHAPTER 1
SPRING FEVER HITS MARLA

Springtime in Richmond, Virginia rolls in before you know it. Just a month ago, the temperature stayed around forty degrees during the day. At night, it would drop ten degrees. Chilly evenings still didn't prevent club-goers, prostitutes and the drunks from coming out. We had days that were definitely meant for making babies or at least days we should have been trying. Couples showed more love and engaged in more conversation during the winter months than any other time of the year. Days filled with snow and ice forced couples to stay inside. It was too cold to go out looking for an extra body or to dress like you were looking for someone to have fun with. That's right, everyone kept their asses inside.

Ah, then came the spring; that damn time of the year when everything and everyone gets loose. Hormones start to rise just as the temperature does. Women come out showing half of their assets and men start running to the gym. Husbands start volunteering to do the grocery shopping, especially on the first of the month. Why? Because their horny asses know it's the first of the month when pussy comes running through the store. Everybody's getting paid on the first, which means plenty of ass is being given up. A man's dick gets hard just going from aisle to aisle, watching asses shake as the women shop. The funny part is watching the men leave the store with phone numbers and a hard dick, anticipating and plotting for a spring fling. Some dumb ass gets into his car and remembers that he didn't get what he came for. There is someone at home anxiously waiting for groceries and he has to run back in and actually shop. Ladies, I didn't forget about you. Those of you without a man, love that day because you want a man and are hoping for just not any man. You want a working man. You figure he'll be in the store dressed handsomely or in a uniform. It doesn't matter what uniform, just something that says he's getting paid. So what do you do? You make sure you're dressed well, and that your assets will be seen. It's payday; men want a little ass and women want to get paid. The thing is, it ain't just the people showing signs of spring fever; the outside animals done lost their damn minds too. Dogs all on each other's backs, cats purring like their fur are being scratched and those damn rabbits fucking like sex is going out of style. If you take a ride through the country and look out in the fields, you may see a huge Angus cow throwing dick to a heifer. If you stay there long enough, the male cow is doing what most men wish to do, fucking everything in sight and nobody's arguing.

Spring time even got to me. On a horny scale between one and ten, I would be a fifteen. On a windy day, my nipples would point like they were giving directions. I think I even started giving off a horny scent. Men started smiling more and their eyes seemed to speak more than words ever could. They were just as hot as I was.

On a bright and sunny Saturday, I woke up feeling like a million dollars. I decided to run out to the local Wal-Mart around lunch time. I slid into an ankle length sundress that swayed along with my ass every step I took. Just as I had anticipated, I arrived to a very crowded parking lot. I parked my car in the back of the parking lot, hoping no one would park beside me and bump my ride. Besides, just in case I saw a man, the walking distance would give him plenty of time to watch how my ass shakes. People were all over the store, children screaming and parents yelling and cursing louder than their brats. Walking, I thought to myself, I needed to get my shit and leave as soon as possible. No way was I going to see a man in this place today with all this chaos. Low and behold, just as I was standing in line, I heard a familiar voice.

He said, "Marla Johnson, is that you?"

I turned around and damn! There stood Paul Dandy Jr., the finest damn man I had ever seen. I met him in my younger days growing up in Varina, Va. We hugged and chatted a little bit. I could have sworn I felt his dick swollen, but hey it was probably my imagination. I had the biggest crush on him back in high school. I was hoping he'd be the one to take my virginity, but it didn't work out that way. He graduated two years before me, and unfortunately, I wasn't dating until after he left for college. Damn shame, I wanted his ass. I could tell by the smile he wore on that handsome face that he wanted to say more than he was able to. I offered him my business card and told him that I would be coming to Surry for a visit in two weeks. I was taking a mini vacation and coming to see my parents. He took the card and as I grabbed my bags to leave, he said, "Marla, I will be calling you when you come home." I smiled a sexy smile and said, "I will be looking forward to hearing from you." I wanted to say, "I will be looking forward to fucking you." I walked to my car, telling myself to calm the fuck down. Just that quick, I was horny as hell. Over the next two weeks we spoke almost daily. We basically started becoming reacquainted with each other and eased our way into some serious flirting.

Two weeks later, I arrived at my parent's house on a Friday and what can I say, he called that night. Of all things, he used my job as an excuse to contact me. He wanted to meet with me about selling some property for him since he realized I was a realtor. Anxiously, I woke up on Saturday morning more than ready to meet him. I knew this meeting was not about business, no matter what he said. I dressed very comfortably for the meeting.

I turned onto a dirt path; at least it appeared that way. The sign clearly read Dandy Road. I really thought it was strange that he wanted to talk business. Everyone knew his family never sold or leased their property. That was how they became wealthy. Some people have money and some have land. In my opinion, either one will guarantee you eat every day. I am cruising down this so called road at about five mph and the freaking dirt and dust is flying up on my BMW. I loved my car, smooth ride just the way I like my man with the exception of a few bumps now and then. Damn, I had just washed it. By the time I reached my destination, I assumed the barn had been about 1.5 miles off the road. This is what I called privacy. I stopped where the instructions told me to. He said he would be working out in the hay barn. I tooted my horn and out stepped one fine ass man. Standing 6'2, dark like the Black Angus cows he was raising, I could only hope his dick hung like one. Old worn faded jeans, bulging at the crotch, with no shirt showing his smooth hair washed in sweat lying across his chest. Everything was cut up, six pack style.

He defined the term country man. You just don't see this in the city. Hard work created this spectacular masterpiece. His smile would guarantee him a spot on the Colgate commercial. Was it my imagination or were his eyes dancing at the sight of me in my "call for a fucking" dress? Seeing the sweat on his chest plunged my mind into dirty thoughts. Watching him walk toward me, my eyes went directly to his manhood. Damn, he just might be built like his male Angus cow. I could feel my pussy, Sheila, start to throb. She had a mind of her own; she started leaking out her love walls. This was not good. I had no panties on so my thighs were getting warm. "Get yourself together, this isn't a social call," I said to myself. I tried to tell myself this was business, but looking at him, I wasn't that stupid. Today had finally come; I was finally gonna fuck him. Just the thought of it made my pussy start knocking. This was on his terms at his place of choice. That was cool, I just wanted him. It really didn't matter if it happened out in the field at this point. His sexy country ass reached my car and opened the door with his "I am so good" smile.

I said hello and stepped out showing all of my 5'8 and one hundred forty lbs. sexy self. I decided to wear a pink spring dress with spaghetti straps that came a few inches above my knees. The white heels I picked out really accentuated my legs. I try to keep in shape by running at least four days a week. This allows everything to stay firm and in place. My hair is always natural, cut in a short style. I keep my hair short for one particular reason. I like to fuck and don't have time to stress over my hair. I got out of the car and he pulled me against his sweaty physique. He kissed me lightly while taking one hand and rubbing the inside of my thighs beneath my dress. He pulled his hand up to his nose and smiled at me. I started getting weak from wanting him. He smiled and licked each finger slowly one by one. He was turning me the fuck on. This definitely wasn't going to be business after all.

I looked at him and said, "I wasn't called for business, I assume."

He looked at me with horniness in his eyes and a sneaky smile on his face. "Naw, this isn't about business or that mental affair bullshit you mentioned on the phone."

"Wow! Somebody wants to fuck! No problem. I want the same thing. However, you are not available to engage in such an activity." I said teasingly.

"Hold up, you are the one that wants me to be a faithful man. I think I should be concerned with that, not you. Don't get me wrong, being faithful is the way it should be. You know as well as I know, we have been attracted to each other for a long time. Had you not moved away, things would be a lot different with us today," he said with that sexy smile.

Laughing, I turned around, pulled the keys out of the ignition and placed them on the seat, proceeding to close the car door.

"Come in the barn where it's cooler, we need to talk." He took my hand and we walked toward the barn. I was feeling excited and confused. We joked a lot about how we wanted each other but knew we couldn't, he was married. So, I suggested to him that one day we should just have a mental affair. He laughed but I explained to him that playing with myself, while thinking about the right person can be an awesome thing. He continued to laugh.

As we entered the barn, things seemed to have gotten more serious. I really wasn't up for conversation. Hell, conversation could come later, after we fucked. My only concern was him hitting this ass and relieving me of this spring fever.

All of a sudden a look of seriousness came across his face.

"I want you so bad that my dick aches just thinking about you," his voice came up a notch. "Don't tell me about my marriage, or being faithful. I want you badly." He started walking toward me.

I began to back up. I found myself backing into a bale of hay, so I stopped. The massive door to the barn was wide open and you could hear nothing this far back. Ahh, there was such peacefulness, no noise of traffic or people for miles. It was just Paul and I, all alone.

"I guess you are ending this mental affair." I said teasingly.

"Stop playing; tell me some other reason why we can't try just once. What is it? You want us to be married? Is that it?"

"Hold on Paul, you know me. It isn't always about love, you being mine or me being yours. I want you. Believe me, this isn't easy. I think we both want that ultimate high, that sexual gratification of fucking someone that we have always wanted, someone that should be off limits. What's that saying? Oh, I know, sins of the flesh. It's in us; temptation. You are married and I want you; that's a sin."

He stepped forward bent down and without speaking, placed a hand beneath my dress on each thigh, rubbing slowing upward. This man was turning me on. He was taking my breath causing me to get weak. He pushed my dress up over my stomach and smiled. He put a finger inside my pussy and it was moving around as if it was dancing.

"Ah!" I gasped and he looked up.

"Something wrong?"

"No, no… nothing at all."

So he took that same finger and slowing sucked on it like he tasted the best thing since sweet potato pie.

His light brown eyes seemed to shine. By now, he knew I didn't have panties on. Here in this barn, we were finally going to have each other. He bent down while pushing my dress up more. He ran his hands across my tummy like he was mesmerized. Peering down at the top of his head, the thrills from his tongue licking the inside of my thighs took over me. I could have sworn I heard the wind blowing the rocks in the driveway with every stroke his tongue made on my thigh. I could not believe it was this good. This was it; I could feel my heart beating faster. I opened my legs wider, begging for him to bring me to my climax.

"Oh Paul, I want you so bad." I moaned while holding my breath and forcing myself to breathe out. He looked up.

"I want you too. Relax, let me show you that a mental affair isn't shit compared to this."

His mouth reached Sheila; his big strong sweaty hands were now making their way to my breasts. He was rubbing my breast and sucking on my clit. I could hear the wind get louder. I could feel my body aching for his every touch. I thought to myself, what is going on? I never ever felt like this. His long thick tongue felt smooth as it made its way through my tunnel. I sat there being tongue fucked and started to shake. He was sucking on Sheila like he wanted to swallow it.

"Right there, just like that. Ooh yes, please Paul don't fuckin stop." I was begging now. That breeze outside got louder. Paul looked up as my body started trembling and just as my pussy started to squirt hitting his nose and forehead, we heard the horn. I came in a powerful way with him. "Beep, Beep," the loudest horn I ever heard. We both jumped, sweaty, exhausted, and filled with desire. He looked up shocked with moist lips and a shiny chin.

"Paul, Paul, honey where are you?" his wife yelled out getting closer to the door.

"Paul, I wanted to surprise you with lunch." She continued to yell.

I sat there stunned, relieved, and shocked. Paul didn't have any time to clean my juices off his face. He just sat there staring at his wife.

****

2 Months Later

I drove past that familiar driveway, a path I yearned to turn onto. Each time, I saw it, my pussy would cry out with an aching. That day, two months ago will remain in my memory. I didn't care about his wife. I still don't care about her, but I will respect her and their marriage. I will respect them until he calls again.

CHAPTER 2
CANDY NEEDS HER FIX

Candy needed her fix. Alcohol, nicotine, nor drugs were anything that Candy desired. Her fix was getting her groove on. Candy was trying to live right, meaning behave, not bother any man that was married. There was just one problem with that, she had fallen in love once and was badly hurt. So she decided because someone had tempted her man, why not dish out payback. Candy was a teacher and loved her students. She found herself being attracted to some of the fathers. There had been some mothers she would have loved to have also. Ever since she could remember, she wanted to teach children. She never planned on picking fathers to fool around with. Candy actually enjoyed seeing parents involved in their child's life.

However, when she met her student, Scotty's parents, she was deeply affected by the way the wife treated the husband. She could see from just having one meeting with them, their marriage was troubled. Malcolm Davis, the father seemed like such a nice man. His looks weren't bad either, as matter of fact, the man was fine as hell. He sat side by side with his wife during the conference. At one time, he reached over to touch her leg and she slyly brushed his hand aside. Malcolm looked hurt and embarrassed at her display in public. When they walked into the classroom, Candy thought what a cute couple. Mrs. Davis, light complexion, about

5'5" with short curly hair. She appeared to be a professional woman; her attire gave hints that she was very confident. Her red suit and red pumps suggested a woman that was powerful and comfortable with herself. Her husband looked very familiar. He stood beside her, standing at least 6'2" tall and weighed no more than about one hundred seventy five pounds. He was dressed in some khaki pants, a pink button down shirt and had the sexiest smile to complement his deep brown complexion. He was clean shaven and very personable. So personable that Candy could tell his wife wasn't pleased with it. Every time Mr. Davis would try to speak with that sexy northern accent, she would over talk him causing him to frown with disgust. Candy updated them on Scotty's academics and told them that their son was destined for success and she enjoyed having him as a student.

Once the meeting came to a close, they all stood up and shook hands. Candy paused a bit when Mr. Davis shook her hand. While saying good bye, he had held her hand and ran his fingers in the inside of her palm and smiled directly at her. Mrs. Davis must have noticed the smiled because her tone changed when she started to walk off and said, "Let's go Malcolm."

Once they were out of the classroom, Candy mumbled, "Well aren't you a cold bitch? Ah and Mr. Davis wants a piece of Candy. Well, I'll have to see what can be done about that." Candy started laughing to herself as she gathered her things to leave for the day.

Candy was a go getter and Mr. Davis wanted to be got. As Candy walked to her car, she smiled at the fact that it was spring time and her body felt the best during this season. She assumed spring affected everyone in this way. But thinking about the couple that she just met with, spring hadn't affected Mrs. Davis and Candy wondered why the hell not with that fine ass man by her side. Shit, Candy felt her girl start to throb when he tickled the palm of her hand. This is why she thought she should invest in panty liners. Her pussy had a mind of her own, horniness would hit Candy so bad at times, that she felt like crying. Candy detested having an ache and not being filled with somebody's manhood. If some women didn't know how to treat their man, Candy decided she would be the fixer. Fixer meaning fix or repair what a man like Malcolm needed worked on. Some men just needed a smile, to have their ego stroked and some just needed to be allowed to release the buildup.

Candy was hoping Malcolm needed something to dump his build up in. If that was the case, the fixer was on her way. Candy had changed into her running clothes, so she headed straight to the park. Running always helped relieve some of the ache and she loved how it kept her body in great shape.

During the next few weeks, Candy discovered two things. She realized Mr. Davis was familiar because she had been seeing him at the track. The second thing was she learned that he was there every day at the same time during the week. She had come to a final decision; Malcolm Davis would be fucked and fucked well. If Mrs. Davis was that cold in public, she sure as hell was ice in the bedroom. Candy thought how pitiful it was that a woman didn't know to keep personal issues private. Now it was up to Candy to brighten her man's world.

Bam! No Panties needed!

It's Friday evening and Candy as usual prepared to go out to the park. However, she would not be running around the track today. She had an itch that needed to be scratched and decided days ago, Malcolm would be the one to scratch it. She went home and changed into something more suitable for this special occasion. After she showered and dressed, she stood there admiring how blessed she was to have the body she had. She loved standing 5'11" tall and carrying one hundred forty lbs. which included a small firm ass tagging along. She was dressed in a small pink low cut tank top with a lace bra and a short white mini skirt that almost showed her goodies. She decided that was cool, because she was headed directly to Malcolm and would not make any stops on the way. She stepped into a pair of open toe sandals with a small heel showing off her pretty feet.

"Looking good Candy." she told herself out loud. She grabbed her bag, turned off the lights and picked up her car keys on the way out the door. She turned onto the long driveway and proceeded to follow it to the far end of the park. The track ran directly toward the parking lot where she planned to wait. Looking at the time on her cell phone, she realized she was on time. Malcolm would be approaching in the next ten minutes. While waiting she checked her hair and her lips and decided all was good. Five minutes before his arrival, she decided to step out of the car. She smiled because she loved the spring and she was looking sexy. It was 6pm in the evening and the trees around the park provided a cool atmosphere. Candy stood there, waiting patiently while trying to keep her horniness level under control. On the way over, she started to play with her clit on the drive but decided against it. She saw him coming down the running trail, looked at her watch and said, "Right on time."

She stood there looking at her tire as if something was wrong when Malcolm stopped a few feet from her. She turned around as if she was surprised to see him there. Malcolm stood there with sweat running down his face and across his masculine chest. He was only in white Nike shorts and sneakers. Candy was turned on immediately. Malcolm stood there wondering how she could be so sexy. He wondered what she would look like if she took her hair out of that bun. Malcolm smiled at her.

"Hey Mrs. Bailey. Is everything okay?"

"Oh yeah, I just pulled back here to get a piece of mind after deciding not to run or play tennis today. How are you?" She didn't feel the need to ask about his wife. She was not concerned with her nor did she want bringing up her name to ruin what she was planning.

"Also, I thought I ran over some glass earlier, so I decided to check my tires." She turned around toward the tires and instead of squatting down, she step back from the tire almost as if she was going to back her ass up on Malcolm. He stood there staring at her ass in the short skirt. Just as she bent over (as if touching her toes) her skirt rose and Malcolm's dick was immediately alerted. He stood there; his heart started racing a little more as he stared at the sweetest, smoothest, plumpest ass he had ever laid eyes on. She bent over never touching the tire, touching her finger tips on her toes. She just hung there as if she was comfortable. It was long enough to give Malcolm a view of part of the pussy being offered. He stood there and cleared his throat, frozen in position. Sweat start to run down his face again. He clenched his hands into fists to prevent from touching her.

Candy looked up at him, "Well Malcolm am I hanging over for nothing?"

Still standing there trying to be strong, wanting to walk away, his feet felt like they had bricks on them. He pleaded with himself to do the right thing. His dick was saying, *Malcolm just touch it, a little bit*. Candy had patience and was in very good shape. She didn't mind hanging for a minute or two. Especially when she looked up at his pants, she saw what was swelling and knew she picked the right man.

Malcolm stepped up a little and placed each hand on her ass cheeks and squeezed them. He then took his hands back and reached down, deep down and brought all ten inches out. Excited and hard as hell, he popped her ass and stepped up closer. This time pushing the skirt up a little more, he took his manhood and ran it up and down the center of her ass a couple of times. Within the next minute, he was entering what felt like a nice little bowl of warm soup on a cool night. He grabbed her around the hips and drove his ten inches inside of her like a mad man. She flinched a little and without thinking of where he was, Malcolm hit it a few times and then pulled her up, and laid her against the car. She spreaded her legs and he pushed his dick up in her as far as he could. She started raining on his dick and down her thighs.

Candy could feel with each stroke his dick diving into the depths of her. They both forgot where they were and started making loud sounds. Candy started feeling herself about to cum while Malcolm thought he was going to lose his mind. They both came together as Malcolm slammed into her harder. Once they finished, Malcolm fell against her on the car allowing his dick to lie against her smooth, firm ass. He reached around her waist feeling down below to see if it was still there and whispered in her ear, "I want more."

Candy reached for a towel in the car and handed it to Malcolm. He stood there staring at her while cleaning himself off.

"We can do this again. Just not today." she said.

"Oh. I understand, you remembered I'm married. I'm sorry, this should not have happened.

I need to be getting home anyway." he said.

"Well I was just going to suggest....well never mind. Thanks, Malcolm." she said while getting in the car.

"Okay, well take care. My car is right over there. See you later." he walked away.

Candy pulled off thinking, "Damn, it wasn't about you being married. I was going to suggest my place."

Malcolm was the one that could make a girl loose her damn mind. A week later, Malcolm couldn't get her off his mind. He decided one weekend to tell his wife he was going out to the bar with some old classmates that were in town. It was a bold lie. But what's a man to do when he runs into Candy? Fuck her is the only option! That's exactly what he did and got fucked right back.

Sins of the Flesh

Malcolm headed straight to the hotel after work. On the way, he made a stop to pick up a few things. Ever since the previous week, when Candy found him in the park, he could not stop thinking about her. That wasn't the best thing because he constantly had to push his dick down in his pants. Malcolm could have sworn his dick never got as hard in his life as it did when Candy bent over in front of him displaying that beautifully shaven pussy. He liked that, his wife's was pretty but he didn't get to see it that much and one thing he wish she would do is get rid of the pussy hair. Pussy covered in hair like it was 1979. Yes sir, he realized he liked a bald pussy, nicely shaved and soft. He daydreamed constantly about releasing his nut on it and having her take her finger and rubbing across it and then he imagined her licking her fingers. Hell, he couldn't wait for this meeting, he had called her at school and simply instructed her on where to come and when. Pussy might be the bomb, but a man still had to be in control at least until Candy took him into her mouth.

Malcolm resided in Petersburg, VA and didn't want to travel too far because he was anxious to get that ass. A week had been too long. His wife had the pussy on lock down. That shit had gotten old. He got a room close to home, Colonial Heights. In his mind, if his wife was worried about him cheating, she'd give up the ass. This was the first time in ten years he cheated. He thought once he was married, pussy would be plentiful. Somebody should have warned him, you get married and then the wife thinks pussy is a privilege not a husband's right. Well Malcolm wanted to yell, "It's my right if you don't want me getting some from a stranger." But he just went on trying to be happy getting it once every two weeks. No more, Candy had opened a new door and damn if he didn't want to be the person to enter.

He drove interstate 95 north toward Colonial Heights, and turned off on South Park Blvd. He parked in the rear of the parking lot trying to be under cover but right about now, he didn't give a damn. His dick was hard and he wanted her underneath him. He got out of the car, looked around and went to the trunk. He knew they only had a few hours but he need his black bag. He stood there and stared at the bag.

Malcolm had no idea she was sitting in the car watching him and was turned on by what she saw. There he was standing at his trunk in a pair of Levis, tee-shirt fitting tightly showing his abs off. He was definitely a sight for a woman's eyes. The Levis showed off his muscular build and that cute little ass of his. For a minute, he contemplated about what he was trying to do with this woman; his son's teacher at that. His dick told his conscious to take the evening off. Malcolm grabbed the bag and headed inside to the front desk.

This was a beautiful hotel and the old woman at the front desk didn't seem too friendly. *Oh well*, Malcolm thought to himself, *not even her old ass was going to ruin his mood.* He thanked her once he had paid and received the key. Malcolm, carrying his bag closely went to the elevator. Before stepping onto the elevator, he used the number Candy had given him and texted the room number to her. He stepped into the elevator smiling, looking forward to her arrival and what he had planned.

Candy sat there thinking about how he gave her the gold at the park. This man was someone that she was excited about fucking again. She never tried to make a habit of making anyone think they were having some long term affair. In Candy's eyes, the excitement was the newness of a man. She didn't want to know what he was going to do before he did it. Besides, she wasn't trying to fall in love. That, she thought was for the wife. She waited for him to enter the hotel before getting out of the car.

Just as fast as he entered she received the room number via text message. Candy smiled at the message and checked her hair, lips, and eyes in the mirror. One of the things she loved most was her young innocent look. People love Candy, well the men did anyway. Today she had decided to remove her hair out of the tired ass bun she wore to school. Her long wavy hair fell out of the bun. She figured she'll enjoy it now because she had an appointment to cut if off and try something new.

So Candy grabbed her purse and keys to exit the car and remembered she needed something out of the glove compartment. She grabbed her lubricant oil and put in inside her purse. She never had a problem with dryness but just in case. Her problem was wetness flowing like a damn river when she'd cum. She strutted in her heels, showing long brown legs. She had changed after school into something more comfortable. Being as though it was spring time temperatures, she put on a short sleeveless sundress that hit a little above her knees and showed a little cleavage to catch a man's eye. Candy loved her body, treasured her body and loved the way men loved it too.

She walked through the doors of the hotel and could feel eyes following her as she walked pass the men standing near the front desk to the elevator. She excitedly stepped on the elevator and press four. She was so horny the number four made her think of Malcolm behind her on all fours. She smiled because she felt her pussy wanting to become friendly and she hadn't even gotten to the room yet. Standing on the elevator she couldn't resist, she stuck a finger inside her panties and put it to her nose and smiled. "That a girl, fresh pussy always the best."

She arrived at the door and for moment was a little thrown off. There was a paper attached to the knob saying do not disturb. She pulled her phone out of her purse and checked the message once more. Yes, she definitely had the right room so she knocked softly.

Malcolm answered the door displaying that Colgate smile. Candy thought to herself, *he had the prettiest white teeth to be a pussy eater.* That gave her comfort, in knowing no germy mouth was worth her picking up infection, no matter how good he could eat the pussy.

"Hey. Come on in." Malcolm said feeling his dick get harder as he watched those legs walk into the room.

"Hey Malcolm, how are you?" Malcolm looked out in the hall; he didn't see anyone and closed the door. He put on the top lock just in case.

"I was okay at first, better now that you are here." He walked over to her showing his bare abs. He had decided to get comfortable and had removed everything but his Levis. Candy could tell he wanted her. That bulge in his pants wanted air. Candy couldn't help but notice the strap lying across the bed and what appeared to be a small rag and a small set of beads beside it.

She looked back at Malcolm and smiled. "I assume those are for us." Hot damn, she looks excited about the extras for the evening.

"Yeah, I thought we would have some fun."

Candy placed her purse on the table and moved closer to the bed. She stepped out of her heels and started to undo her dress, but he stopped her.

"Please let me unzip it." he step toward her and she turned her back to him. Malcolm unzipped it and ran a finger down the center of her back. He couldn't help but appreciate the smoothness of her skin and he leaned over to kiss her neck. She smelled of a sexy scent, nothing cheap but sexy like the woman that wore it. As he kissed her neck lightly, Candy felt a chill run through her. His lips were soft and it felt like a slight breeze ran across her neck. Malcolm lifted his head and continued to unzip her. By the time he got to her butt, he realized that she had on the sexiest red thongs. His dick was about to explode. As Candy stood there waiting for him to remove the dress she felt his lips right above her butt, kissing with tenderness. He then pulled the dress over her head slowly. He turned her around to him, and gently inserted his tongue into her pretty little mouth. The kiss alone got her girl below all stirred up. There she stood in just thongs and she wondered when he would remove those. She was ready to be fucked in the most urgent way. When he stopped and looked at her, she decided it was time to undo his jeans. She touched the print of his dick outside the jeans and unzipped them. He went to take his manhood out.

Moving his hand to the side, Candy whispered, "No, let me."

She proceeded to take it out and heard him sigh. She assumed he was uncomfortable in that trap and very hard. As he took over and removed his boxers and jeans, she lowered herself down on her knees. Candy licked her lips and slowly kissed the head, and then licked his dick slowly down toward the balls. She took a ball at a time and licked and then sucked softly. She could hear his breathing was increasing. She licked upward and then without notice, she took his dick into her mouth and held onto it while sucking on it. He was about ten inches, which was cool because she was a deep throater. She started sucking on it and each time he entered her mouth, he'd moan.

After about two minutes, she looked up and said, "I bet you can't spell your name."

"What? I can spell my name." he was wondering what the hell was going on, his dick was throbbing.

"I know you can silly, but I mean I bet you can't spell it before I cause you to nut all in my mouth."

"Let me try. You think you that good? Huh?"

Next thing he knew she said, "Go." Candy pulled on his dick and he started.

"M...a."

She pulled more pushing saliva around in her mouth.

"M...a...m"

She started sucking a little faster and licked around the head after each time she let up off his dick. Malcolm was still trying.

"M..a...m...a..llll," he was stuttering and trembling and just as he said, "c" his dick spit out and Candy was there catching it, like it was the last of a fine wine.

Malcolm took a minute to recover and seeing her lick the last drops off her lips turned him on more. His dick started to swell all over again. This woman was trying to break a brother down, he thought to himself. But soldiers don't quit and once a Marine always a Marine.

With a sudden burst of energy, he picked her up and laid her on the bed close to the headboard. Candy felt excited and turned on to the highest. When she saw the sheer glaze over his eyes, she got hotter and decided to let him have his way. Malcolm got on the bed and leaned over her. He grabbed her hands gently and put them over her head and tied them to the headboard. Candy laid there feeling her pussy getting wetter at the thought of what he was going to do. She watched as Malcolm picked up the rag and the beads.

"Trust me, I won't hurt you."

Candy smiled and said, "Well I hope you hurt me a little."

That statement made him feel like he could fuck her all night long. Malcolm brought the rag to her mouth and without saying anything, Candy opened wide. A freak for sure, Malcolm thought to himself.

"You had fun with your little "spell my name" game, so I want to play now." he said as he placed the rag gently inside her mouth. Candy laid there bound and gagged, with an ache in her pussy that was bringing tears to her eyes. She laid there watching his every move. It wasn't fear but excitement, his dick was hard and extremely thick. Malcolm opened her legs and could see the juices laying on the surface of her entrance. He leaned down and ran his tongue from her clit down to her hole. Candy moaned and squirmed a little. He looked at her and her pretty brown skin and smiled. He sat up and rose both of her legs up, bending them at the knees and separating them. He picked up the line of small beads and inserted slowing inside her honey hole. She could feel the build up from his touch and inserting the beads.

Once Malcolm had them in, he rubbed his dick and said to her, "not now, just a little longer." and placed his head between her legs. He started licking and sucking on her clit, while he could hear her moan. He licked down the clit into her hole and tasted the sweet juices that were starting to leak. He paused and pulled a bead out slowly, another slowly and she was pleading with each moan he heard. Then he blew into her hole a soft breath and went back to pressing his tongue on her pussy more. Her body started shaking and legs were starting to fall and he knew it was time to bring her home. He pressed his tongue against her with pressure and with a hand; he removed the rest of the beads slowly. He looked up and there she was helpless, crying and very satisfied.

He wasn't done. Hell no, this pussy was meant to be taken by a man, a fucking Marine. He removed the rag and undid the straps. Candy was breathing hard, and before she could say anything, he picked her up and placed her on his lap as he sat back on the bed. Candy sat down on his dick with excitement. There was a little pain from his hardness and once she was on it, she could feel the head touching her g-spot. She started moving up and down slowly looking him directly in his eyes. As she moved, she said, "This is what you call a game, a teasing game." She moved a little faster and then she slowed her pace and moved her hips in a circular motion and just when he moaned more, she reached over and put the rag in his mouth. She rode him harder and harder and just as she was about to come, he moaned and they came together. Candy fell, exhausted and satisfied, on top of him and removed the rag.

Together they both said, "Damn."

Candy got up and walked over to her bag. When she returned to Malcolm, she handed him the lubricant. He looked puzzled until she went to the other side of the bed and turned her back to him and spread her legs as her feet touched the floor. Candy bent over and Malcolm's dick stood up again.

CHAPTER 3

UNFUCKING BELIEVABLE

Meanwhile, outside on a busy New York City street, anxious friends stood waiting to enter Zoey's. It was different from most weekend nights. Tonight Zoey had decided she would throw a party to celebrate friendships and the list involved rather interesting people. Her friendships included people of all races and religions. Zoey was just a very loving person. Tonight would also be the last night to spend with her dear friend Meisha. Zoey was trying not to get too emotional behind Meisha leaving town. But at the same time, she was excited to see her best friend, Sebastian; he was another friend Zoey had met in college.

Although, their friendship started right after Meisha left college in their sophomore year, Zoey and Sebastian had classes together and a friendship was formed instantly. Zoey never looked at Sebastian in a dating way. They were just platonic friends. Zoey did however think on more than one occasion, Meisha and Sebastian would make a great pair. But for some reason, whenever Zoey would go to meet Meisha, Sebastian always had plans. She would tell him, she knew the one woman that would loosen him up. He was always talking about how he was going to be so successful in the family business and college came first, love would have to wait. Well he proved it to be true and now since graduation, she finally would get to introduce him to Meisha. Zoey was more than excited to have all her friends in one place and perhaps create a love connection.

Four days before the party, he had only come to the city because Maximillian's ass claimed to be too busy at one of their banks. Sebastian didn't believe him. Max's ass didn't want to come because he had no freakin' life. All he wanted to do was sit in that damn office and work. He knew coming to the city, he would have to attend meetings, socialize and attend dinners. Sebastian didn't mind so much as coming to the city. He loved socializing but he wasn't thrilled about attending meetings all week. But one good thing that he looked forward to was Zoey's party on Friday.

Zoey had called him a week before and as luck would have it, he would be there in the city that very same week. Zoey seemed really happy to know that they would be seeing each other after two years. Monday had been a busy day, meeting with clients as he expected it would be. Sebastian felt worn out from the plane ride the previous day and getting settled in his hotel room. Nancy, his sister always took care of things like his hotel stay and transportation. Just as he was about to meet with his last group of people, someone caught his attention.

He was walking rather fast, trying to reach the elevator before the doors closed. He stepped in and without looking out to see if anyone else was coming, he pushed the 5th floor button. Suddenly a tall, medium brown skinned woman rushed in holding a large bag in one hand and stopping the elevator with the other hand.

Mumbling out loud, "Damn, rude ass people. Can't even hold the fuckin door for a minute." Meisha was surprised to see a tall sexy white male staring at her. Then she looked up at Sebastian and was suddenly speechless.

He was standing their wondering, who was this feisty sexy ass woman who had just stepped into his life. Well actually stepped into the elevator he thought to himself. She took a small step and leaned toward the panel and pressed level five. "Excuse me," she said. As she was speaking, he couldn't help but glance down at her long legs standing in the sexiest pink stilettos he'd ever seen with a brown skirt that was just above the knee showing just enough of her thighs for one's imagination.

"No problem, bad day?" he asked wishing she could have stayed leaned over for a few more seconds, just enough to have seen more of what looked like lovely brown breasts in that low cut pink sweater.

"Sort of bad. Just so much going on at once," she said smiling at him.

Just as he was about to introduce himself, the damn bell dinged and the doors of the elevator opened. She stepped off just as quickly as she had come on. So he stepped out and stood there for a minute watching her walk toward her destination. All he kept thinking to himself was *who was that woman?* When he glanced toward her breast in that sweater, he felt himself swelling below. What a wild reaction toward a perfect stranger with a foul mouth. Laughing he went in the opposite direction to his last meeting of the day. The meeting didn't last long; he basically had to provide individuals with the numbers his bank was prepared to offer in securing their company's banks.

Once the meeting had ended, he walked with a good friend he had attended college with toward the elevators. The friend needed to stop by his office before leaving. As they turned the corner, Sebastian saw her again. This time she was leaning over the secretary's desk.

"Here we go again," he thought. His dick was starting to act up again. This day had not only been busy but he had suddenly been fighting to hold down his manhood. He really needed to get back to the hotel and have a drink.

He looked to his friend and asked, "Who is that woman over there?"

Following the direction of Sebastian's finger, Daryl said, "Her name is Meisha"

"Ah, Meisha. What exactly does Meisha do here?" Sebastian asked curiously.

"She actually works for your sister." Daryl said.

"Nancy? What does she do for Nancy? Where is she from?" Laughing, Sebastian said, "Sorry too many questions at once. Take your time, answer all of them."

This time Daryl started laughing with him. Daryl stared at Meisha while speaking to Sebastian. Sebastian wasn't sure why Daryl had started staring at her with a wishful look. He suddenly looked like a child about to beg for candy.

"Well, Nancy sent us word months ago, that her right hand person would be coming here to start working with HR and others as far as what would happen with the employees here once the bank was purchased."

Sebastian waved his hand, "Go on friend, where is she from?"

"As far as I know she's from your home town." Daryl said still staring at her. "She is one fine ass women. From the first day she arrived, heads have been turning and men have tried and all have failed."

"What? Are you serious? What about you? Everyone tried but you?" asked Sebastian now turning to his friend who was getting a little red in the face.

"Actually, I tried the honest approach, no game playing approach. I approached her like a man."

"And?" Sebastian asked impatiently.

"Well let's just say she is feisty as hell." he laughed.

Okay, she turned me down, but before turning me down, she looked down at me as if I was a child and smiled, said no thanks and walked off."

Sebastian couldn't help but laugh, "come on Daryl, she didn't look down at you like you were a child.

"She looked down because she's about 5'11 and you're about 5'2." Sebastian couldn't help but to laugh as if a joke had been said.

Daryl didn't like it; he looked at Sebastian with a hurt look, "Really man? Really Sebastian, you want to joke on my size? That shit wasn't funny at all. That was a cruel joke."

Sebastian stopped laughing, slapped his friend's shoulder and said, "Aw man, you know I'm just kidding." He started laughing again.

"Okay, seriously man, don't assume she was looking down on you. Don't be getting "little man syndrome" on me.

"Alright, I guess you're right. But I felt real bad. And hell no, I don't get little man syndrome, I know my shit is right." Daryl said poking his chest out, "just because I'm short don't mean I am less of a man. Oh well, her loss."

Sebastian was still laughing when he had reached the elevator. He looked back at Daryl, "Alright man, I'll see you in the morning."

"Okay. Bright and early." said Daryl.

As the doors closed, Sebastian said, "That depends on how my night goes."

Outside the building, Sebastian caught a cab. Now he wished he would have accepted Nancy's offer of a private car for the week. Cabs weren't that bad if you could catch one when you needed it.

The cab pulled in front of the luxurious Four Seasons Hotel New York. Nancy always insisted on staying at the best hotels. This was her favorite out of all the hotels in New York City. Sebastian greeted the doorman and caught the elevator up to his room. A luxurious penthouse welcomed him each and every time he came to the city.

One day he imagined, he would have a wife by his side to enjoy these trips into the city. At forty-two, he still hadn't found the woman of his dreams. The women he often ran into were conceited and cared more about money. He had been raised in a wealthy family but was taught that a bank account didn't make you better than anyone else. He removed his jacket and that awful tie, and walked directly to the mini bar. He poured himself two straight shots of Wild Turkey and downed it. Of course they didn't carry his drink at first, it wasn't their most popular drink among the wealthy, but, they were happy to accommodate when he requested it. "Why not one more," he thought to himself.

He took that one over to sofa and sat there tossing the liquid around in the glass thinking about Meisha. Over and over the scene in the elevator played in his mind. He realized she was just as surprised by him as he was her. Sebastian knew by the way she looked at him, that she felt the same attraction he had felt. He would find her this week and at least ask her out. Damn, he hadn't been that turned on like this in years. How had he missed meeting Meisha? He definitely needed to stay around the home place more. He just could not stand being around his niece, Candy. He felt like that girl has serious problems. He recalled Nancy always saying she didn't needed to travel as much anymore, because Meisha loved traveling.

All of a sudden a thought hit Sebastian, "Is Meisha one of the ladies in Nancy's Roller Coaster club?" He still didn't know what kinds of women were so desperate that they'd join a club to have sex with a stranger.

That was some strange shit to Sebastian. But he always tried not to judge others. He'd have to call his sister, even though she might not tell him. He was certainly hoping Meisha was in the club, because he wanted a membership ASAP. He would be seeking her out before heading back home to Virginia.

****

Meisha

Meisha watched out of the corner of her eye, as the two men stood there talking. The new guy who she'd run into on the elevator was sort of sexy. She felt some sort instant sexual attraction when she was standing beside him. She could tell they were looking at her ass, so she tiptoed a little more to give them a better view. Meisha was used to attention but for some reason she was enjoying the stranger's stare. She could have sworn her pussy had started pulsating but she removed that thought because she was just horny as hell. She had been like this for months. She wasn't sure of his race, he looked Italian, slight tan, shiny black hair that was certainly longer than most men's hair, hanging almost to his shoulders, and funny looking eyes. He appeared to be about 6'3, a big man. Meisha loved big sexy men. This one just happened to be much lighter than most. He was attractive as hell, but she didn't do white men. She needed a big dick, the kind of dick only a brother could give. There it goes again, her pussy throbbed. Damn, whatever stock he came from, he had been well bred. Why was she thinking of this light skinned man?

Once the stranger got on the elevator and Daryl, the little man, walked away, Meisha went to her office to get her things to head back to the hotel. On the ride back to the hotel, Meisha thought to herself, "Just maybe I need to join Nancy's club, after all I don't need to be walking around getting horny at the sight of every big sexy man I see, especially a white man. I just need sex, no strings attached."

Meisha was all for fun but she never did a stranger. That just wasn't on her list of dreams but desperate people tend to do desperate things during desperate times. Nancy's club motto was "For a woman to have a roller coaster ride."

"Hell, I just need to get laid. A quickie would do as long as I get mine," she mumbled to herself. The cab stopped right out front of the Four Seasons Hotel New York and Meisha had to stop her daydreaming. She tipped the driver and proceeded to the door.

She smiled and asked the cute young doorman how he was doing and headed up to her room. She could feel his eyes watching her ass, so she walked a little slower smiling to herself. "Another horny ass man," she thought and stepped on the elevator. Just as Meisha was about to step off the elevator, a man was rushing on and bumped into her. They looked at each other and Meisha was surprised.

"Unfucking believable, you again?" and she started laughing.

This time Sebastian laughed and said, "Is your mouth always that bad?"

A little taken back, Meisha smiled, "Well, not always."

"You could have fooled me," he said laughing.

"Are we staying at the same hotel?" she asked, as her pussy started throbbing again. She certainly hoped his answer was yes. She was thinking tonight she would have to fuck a light skinned man.

"Yes, it appears that we are," he said standing there looking finer than thick T-bone steak.

Meisha's mind was saying, *a steak I would love and I'd love to have a bone to suck dry.* Damn where in the hell did that thought come from. Outside the elevator, Sebastian stood. She stepped off the elevator and he stepped on and pressed hold for the elevator. He extended his hand to introduce himself.

"Hi again, I am Sebastian. I believe you work with my sister Nancy."

Her face lit up, "Yeah. I do work for Nancy. You have a great sister." she held out her hand.

"I'm Meisha." It seemed like it was a couple of minutes before they decided to let go.

"Well, it's nice meeting you. I'm sure we will see each other again. I am here in town for the whole week, "Sebastian said, with a sneaky smile.

"Nice meeting you also. I do hope to see you again to. But no more running into each other at elevators." she smiled.

They both laughed and went their separate ways. On the elevator, once the doors closed, Sebastian spoke out loud, "No more running into each other at elevators, but hopefully we can run into each other in other ways."

As Meisha opened the door to her room, she was hoping she'd see him again and maybe next time, they would have more time to talk."

Sebastian was going down to the hotel's bar to have another drink. He didn't feel like drinking alone after having a few in his suite. He couldn't get this Meisha person off his mind and then he ran into her again. He decided to stop by the hotel desk and get her room information. At first the clerk was reluctant especially since he didn't even know her last name. After reminding the desk clerk of whom he was and telling them that she worked for his sister, he was given the information. He assumed it was the fifty dollar tip that helped too. Once they told him, he had them send someone to her room with a message requesting a meeting over drinks.

Meisha got undress down to her camisole and panties and decided to have a strong drink before showering. She thought about the handsome white man she kept running into. She wasn't racist, but she wondered since when had she ever felt this turned on by the opposite race.

"Oh well, there's a first time for everything. Everyone has the same color blood." She found herself pouring a second drinking and drinking only half of it before completely undressing to step into the shower.

As she showered, she realized no alcohol or shower was gonna remove that stud from her mind. Just as Meisha had stepped out of the shower, she heard a knock at the door. She had no idea who that could be.

There on the outside of the door, stood Sebastian. He decided to cancel the messenger and invite her himself. He didn't think it was the smartest thing to do because he was practically a stranger.

48

But putting smart things aside, his dick had decided that this needed to be handled personally. He had purchased a bottle of the finest whiskey they had and caught the elevator up to her floor.

She got a little excited thinking maybe it was Sebastian, but then thought that was impossible since they hadn't even exchanged information. So she grabbed a towel and wrapped it around her wet body and went to the door.

"Who is it?" she said out loud.

"Sebastian. Nancy's brother, we met earlier." he said suddenly feeling a little nervous and horny.

Meisha paused excitedly wondering why he was at her door, "Oh, hi Sebastian. What do you need?"

He leaned toward the door and said, "Do you really want me to say it... out here in the hall?"

Those words made her pussy get excited. Laughing Meisha opened the door and dropped the towel shocking Sebastian.

"Hell no!" opening her arms she said, "I want you to come inside and tell me." she smiled.

For the first time ever, Sebastian was speechless; he stood there gazing at her medium build with the pretty smooth brown skin. Her nipples were eye catching sticking out from breast that made him

wish he could put one in his mouth. His eyes moved downward.
There, between her legs, a perfect shaven pussy with some sexy
black hair that only runs down the center of her pussy to her clit.
He felt his dick straining to get out and be set free to take on this
feisty bold woman.

"He held out the bottle of whiskey and said, "I got the drink if
you got the glasses."

Meisha stepped aside, never picking up the towel and said,
"Well come on in Sebastian, this isn't for others to see."

Sebastian, all smiles while trying not to jump her bones,
stepped in and handed her the bottle. Unbelievable and sexy was
all he could think of to describe her. Fuck Nancy's club he thought,
he was doing this on his own. Meisha shut the door and walked
toward the kitchen. She also had been given a suite to stay in.
Sebastian followed her naked body into the kitchen. He noticed
even her ass was a beautiful brown, firm and it took everything in
him to control his hands. She was there in front of him completely
naked and barefoot.

In his mind, it didn't get any better than this. He was wondering
to himself if he should just stand there and remove his clothes.
Hey, they both were horny adults and obviously she was going to
let him fuck her but he said over and over, don't show a lack of
self-control. She's leading this, so wait for her to make the move.

His mind was saying, *are you fucking slow? Touch her, grab her, and fuck her! She's fucking naked!!* He ignored his mind and started talking.

"So how was your day at work?" he asked thinking how dumb was that question.

She turned around and took the bottle of whiskey and smiled at him. She opened the whiskey and starting pouring the drinks, contemplating how to answer him. She stepped closer to him, handed him his glass. Once he lifted the glass to his lips, she smiled.

"Really Sebastian? That's your question to me? I thought by our attraction to each other, you wanted to fuck me?"

Sebastian, surprised by her bluntness spit whiskey out all over her breast and felt so embarrassed. He sat the glass down. This was a wild one, he thought to himself. Meisha didn't mean to make him nervous, but couldn't help laughing while Sebastian reached out to wipe whiskey off her breast. Suddenly the laughter stopped and fire ran through her body as he wiped and then started rubbing his thumbs across her nipples as if teasing her. Sebastian thought, to hell with waiting, he wanted her. She placed the glass on the counter. She stood there unable to move and watched those weird eyes of his glaze over her as if he was mesmerized. Meisha had never seen a man as turned on as this. He then stopped and picked her up like a man leaving the church would carry his bride.

"Where?" he asked.

"Bedroom," she whispered still surprised at her boldness with this man.

He headed down the hall because it looked as if their suites were very similar with the floor plans. He reached her room and could smell the flowers that gave such an exotic feeling. She must have specially bought them herself. The aroma in the room created the perfect atmosphere for what was about to happen. Sebastian laid her in the center of the bed, watching her as he undressed.

Neither spoke as no words were needed, they had nothing to speak about. They weren't husband and wife, hell they weren't even friends. They were just two people with a desperate attraction to each other. Sebastian removed his shirt and finally undid his belt and zipper, giving his hard dick a little breathing room. Sebastian leaned toward her and started rubbing his hand up and down her pussy. He inserted his finger and moved it around gently within her walls.

He looked at her and said, "This right here, my feisty MeMe is what I want." He started to move his finger around a little faster, feeling her juices getting warmer. "I want you as wet as you can get; you're gonna need it, to take this gift I want to share."

"Damn," Meisha thought to herself, "when had she told him he could call her MeMe?

But who cares what he calls me, stroking my pussy like this. He can call me bitch and I wouldn't fucking care. Just share the damn gift." She wanted to just fuck like there would be no tomorrow. Sebastian stood up and removed his pants and then his boxers.

"Oh, hell no!" Meisha yelled.

She startled him, although he knew she was surprised. After all, who would think a white guy would have all of this. Now she would know if she didn't already, not to listen to rumors. He stood there and smiled.

"What is it MeMe? Have you changed your mind?"

"Hell no, I just want to say, I can take half but not all!"

Sebastian laughed and let the boxers drop to the floor then lean lightly over Meisha, allowing her to just feel his 11 inch dick against her pussy.

"Don't worry, you say half now but I'm hoping you change your mind. MeMe, you got me so hard, a cat couldn't scratch my dick."

He kissed her gently. He knew why she laughed. It was that saying about his dick. They kissed and Sebastian rose up so he could lower himself in her. He would only give half until she asked for more. Slowly the head touched the entrance that was pushing warm juices out and she moved away a little and then the look on her face said she was ready. He felt the warm heat and slowly he went in and out, each time a little deeper. She was getting hotter and hotter, and before he knew, his feisty friend had grabbed his ass and lifted her body off the sheets to meet him. She started to shout.

"Now! Give me all of it. Fuck me Sebastian!"

It took everything in him not to give it all to her at first. With a swift movement, he drove his dick into her and he felt like a man being pulled at in the middle of a storm. Meisha's pussy muscles were moving off the chart, each time he went a little deeper, her muscles would tighten. Almost as if she wanted to trap this dick inside her. They matched each other's movements like they had been together countless times before. The movement increased more and Meisha let her body fall back against the soaked sheet and held on to his ass as if she was about to fall over a cliff. At once together, they both were sweating, hearts beating fast, they came and they yelled and Sebastian fell on top of her.

She whispered in an exhausted tone, "Unfucking believable." Just then out of nowhere the loudest alarm went off. They looked at each other, jumped and started to get dress.

"That's the fire alarm, let's go Meisha!" Sebastian said while dressing.

"Unfucking believable" Meisha whined.

Laughing, Sebastian grabbed her hand pulling her out the door, "Is that your favorite line?"

Meisha laughed and then turned to him when they got to the steps, "Sebastian, you ain't heard half of my crazy lines."

"I will hold you to that, we're not finished." he said.

"Oh hell no, I know that." she laughed.

Something odd happened before they started down the steps. Sebastian leaned over and kissed her lightly on the lips. He was not finished with that feisty sister. They stared at each other for a second, neither speaking and then headed down the steps out of the building.

People were running down the stairs in no form of order. Every level they reached, more people were crowding on the stairs. Sebastian and Meisha were separated by the time they got outside. Each one scanned the crowd looking for the other. After being outside for almost two hours, police announced that all had been a false alarm. They were told everyone could go in.

Sebastian was one of the last to enter the hotel and headed straight to the front desk. He picked up his messages and noticed an important message to call his sister. He decided he would call Meisha to see if they could finish what they had started, after he phoned Nancy. Sebastian spoke to his sister, and got very agitated at her request, he picked up the phone to call Meisha's room. There was no answer so he assumed she was sleep.

"Damn," he said out loud. He would be leaving in a couple of hours to head back to his bank's main office in Virginia for an important meeting in the morning. There would be no way he would see Meisha again.

He yelled out Meisha's line, "UNFUCKING BELIEVABLE." He called downstairs to have a car ready for his departure. He packed and two hours later he was down at the front desk leaving a note of apology for Meisha. He had no idea if he'd ever see her again. He didn't like this feeling at all. He assumed like any other fling it would fade away. However, he never had a fling with

Meisha. He'd like to pack Meisha, her foul mouth and her snapping pussy in a suitcase and chain it to his wrist.

Meisha headed back her suite, assuming Sebastian would be shortly behind her. She was silently hoping that was not going to be their last time getting together. She stopped by the desk on her way up and picked up her messages. She waited until she reached her room to read the long message Nancy had left. She reached her door and was disappointed that Sebastian was not there and waiting. Nancy had left a message expecting her to wrap things up in New York City within the next week or two. Nancy also said that if she was free, Meisha should look up her brother, Sebastian for dinner or something. She had also given Meisha Sebastian's room number and told her to not let him intimidate her. He tried to be very serious but could be fun also.

Meisha poured her a drink and sat on the sofa laughing. "Wow, Nancy if you only knew. Your brother is definitely fun. No, make that exciting, sexy, and well endowed." Meisha walked back to her bedroom and stood there staring at the wet sheet, her mind went right back to what had transpired hours earlier. She decided to sleep in the smaller room in her suite with the fresh sheets. Besides, if Sebastian came back they could do it all over again. She decided to call his penthouse, but didn't get an answer. She figured he hadn't got back yet.

So she decided to take a shower and prepare herself for him again. Once she finished her shower, she checked her messages and saw none. She assumed he got what he wanted and was gone. That was cool with her; she knew it was just a quick fuck with a stranger. She went to bed thinking about him and had to make herself go to sleep. She tossed and turned all night long and even woke a couple of times to see if he had called.

After three days, she decided it was exactly as she thought; a quick fling. On Friday, she had removed him somewhat from her mind. She was excited about Zoey's friendship party. Saturday, she would be packing to leave and returning home. She was so glad she was able to wrap things up with no problems at the office because she was needed in Virginia.

Her girlfriend, Tracy, had called the night before and sounded very upset. She said something about her husband cheating with her son's teacher. She even said she had a video for proof. Meisha wondered how the hell she got a video. Meisha was anxious to get home to find out.

The last day at the office went smoothly. Meisha was given a going away lunch and told that they had enjoyed having her around. A couple of guys asked for her number but she had said no thanks.

Meisha got back to her suite, showered and dressed. She didn't want to be late for Zoey's party. It was spring and Meisha was feeling good. She dressed to party.

Sebastian had caught a cab straight from the airport after calling the office to see if Meisha was still there. The secretary said that she was heading out for the evening, something about a party at Zoey's Place. Sebastian suddenly thought about the same party he was invited to by his college friend. Then it dawned on him.

Meisha? No way, could she be the friend Zoey has been telling him about for years? Naw. That would be too much of a coincidence. He also called the Four Seasons Hotel to let them know of his arrival. He requested to speak with whoever was in charge of the kitchen. He told the kitchen manager that he wanted fresh strawberries and a bottle of their best wine deliver to his suite and to store both in the refrigerator immediately. He also mentioned that he would be sure to add an extra tip to his bill.

He wasn't sure what time Meisha and him would get back there and if Meisha had other plans. He wasn't concerned with her other plans. She would be spending the night with him. He'd already made that decision. Three days had passed and he had been moody as hell. Nancy and his brother assumed it was the traveling that was wearing him out. He felt like this woman had embedded herself in his mind and his soul.

So here he was at Zoey's big party. Sebastian was glad he changed into casual clothes before catching his flight. He had been so consumed about Meisha and finding her that he completely forgot about the party. Well, here he was and he needed to find Meisha and of course Zoey also. You could see through the large glass window on both sides of the door.

One side showed a bar and folk' dancing like it was New Year's Eve. On the other side of the building, you could see couples and groups of people sitting at tables eating and laughing. *How could one building hold two different scenes,*" he wondered to himself. He took a deep breath before entering the establishment.

He reminded himself that he had come a long way from home to see her. There was no turning back for him. Nancy had tried to insist that he stay in Virginia to help at the bank, but Sebastian said for the first time, "No way!"

He entered the sports bar/restaurant and was amazed at how it appeared to be an upper class establishment. There, in the middle of the entrance, stood a hostess with a bright smile and very white teeth. She appeared to be around twenty one and excited about her job. *Wow*, he thought, to be that young again.

"Hello, welcome to Zoey's Place. Will you be dining or going to the bar area?" she asked showing those bright white teeth.

"I'm not really sure. It will depend on whether you can answer my question? Do you know Meisha; tall, brown skinned female? I was told she....," the hostess interrupted,

"Sure. I know Meisha; Zoey's best friend right? I am sure she's here making everyone laugh as usual," pointing to the right, she continued," "Keep to the right and follow the sound of music. She came in about an hour ago."

Hearing the hostess talk about Meisha making others laugh, caused a jealous feeling. He wanted to be part of Meisha's fun. *Damn where did that thought come from?*"

Sebastian reached the bar, seeing how everyone was having a great time, he decided he'd find Zoey after he found Meisha. He saw her out on the dance floor. Some guy had her pulled close to him and had his hands around her waist. *That's too close to her ass*, he thought. They were moving side to side, keeping up with the beat. *Definitely the wrong damn song playing and the wrong damn kind of dancing.* Sebastian headed straight to the bar and sat down because he felt a strange feeling of jealousy growing. His dick was starting to harden and swell.

The bartender stood there behind the bar talking to him, "What can I get for you?"

"Two shots of Wild Turkey on the rocks, very little rocks," said Sebastian turning his attention back to Meisha and that guy.

"Okay, be right back with your drink," the bartender assumed Sebastian heard him.

Three minutes later, the bartender called to him twice before Sebastian turned around.

He was handed his drink. "Oh! Okay thanks." and pulled out a ten and said, "Keep the change."

Looking directly at Meisha, he took a swallow of his drink. Meisha had been dancing with her eyes closed. He sat there wondering, *was she thinking of him or the man that was holding her so closely*?

Meisha opened her eyes and saw him. She looked very surprised. He loved those sexy light brown eyes of hers. Just as she was leaving the dance floor coming toward him, another song came on. "Motivation, by Kelly Rowland, and the same guy reached for her to dance again.

Sebastian sat the glass down, saying, "Oh hell no. This shit stops now." Meisha was about to start dancing and saw Sebastian walking toward her. He was so sexy; all 6'3 of him and his shoulder length black hair. She couldn't help but think as he was walking, "*Who would ever look at this sexy ass white man and think he was packing such a big dick?* She was so glad she knew he was."

Sebastian reached them and looked at the man and said, "Excuse me but I believe it's my turn."

The man started to say something, but as he was looking up to Sebastian, he realized this chick, no matter how fine, wasn't worth pissing this big man off.

"Cool." the guy said and never looked at Meisha. He was too busy moving out of Sebastian's way.

They both stood there for a moment looking at each other. Sebastian reached for her, placing his long arms around her and she felt his big hands gently squeeze her ass.

"Missed me?" She laughed, "Unfucking believable. Here I thought I wouldn't see you ever again."

"You got to be fucking crazy if you thought that. You work for my sister."

"Sebastian, I have been working for your sister for two years and had never met you."

Sebastian started laughing then, " Well that was then, this is now."

Meisha took the song very seriously and pressed herself closer so that she could feel his hardness up against her. Sebastian was bold and didn't care that they were not the only people there. He moved his hands beneath her skirt and rubbed her ass like he wanted her right there. Kelly's song said, "When we're done, I don't want to feel my legs."

Sebastian looked directly into Meisha's eyes, squeezed her ass a little harder and whispered, "You won't feel your legs, I promise that."

Meisha felt like she could cum right there on the dance floor. Hell, he could fuck her right there and she wouldn't care who saw it. This man brought boldness and excitement. She was going to enjoy this ride even if only for one more night. Sebastian did something that took Meisha totally by surprise. With one hand he held her close, his other hand moved around to the front of her skirt, she felt nervous and hot. He used his fingers to reach inside her panties and started to finger her right there. Her body shivered but she wasn't cold.

Her pussy got so wet she could feel her juice running down the inside of her thighs. His finger was moving all around and it felt like he put two in. Right then, another song was played, a different beat, she leaned on him for support, she was cumming on the middle of the dance floor. Sebastian knew she could barely stand. He removed his hand and licked his fingers and then pulled her close by him, kissed her, and walked off the floor. Meisha could not believe what had just happened. When she looked up, Zoey was standing there with her mouth wide open and her eyes told she had seen something.

CHAPTER 4

A HOE'S KNOCKING AT THE DOOR

You shared everything with your new best friend? Didn't your momma ever tell you that some things you keep to yourself?" Meisha was a straight up and to the point type of girl. She didn't see any reason to sugar coat shit, even when speaking to her girlfriend. She started yelling, but then lowered her voice, shaking her head while thinking to herself, how stupid can this woman be?

"First of all, she isn't my best friend; you are the only best friend I have, smart ass." Tracy yelled back.

Meisha frowned, "I sure as hell can't tell I am still your best friend. We rarely speak on the phone anymore and obviously the time I spent in New York working, prevented me from hearing about all of this crazy shit Jamal done put you through. By the way, all this drama sounds like a freaking reality show." Tracy seemed to be pleading, "Please just be the best friend you have always been and put the crazy remarks to the side, please."

Meisha took a deep breath and released it, wanting to be more calm, "I told you never to trust a man one hundred percent, they all capable of cheating. Even when the strongest are tempted, they can fall. Sounds like you dangled your husband in front of her, the way a trainer dangles a bone in front of a dog. If you hold it out there long enough, the dog will bite. You also said that you heard the teacher was a hoe? Really Tracy, what the hell were you thinking?"

Tracy, wiping the tears from her eyes said, "Meisha, you know you should have been a damn Marine. You speak to me as if I have no feelings. It's as if you don't think this shit is supposed to hurt."

Meisha got up from her chair and joined Tracy on the plastic covered sofa. She hugged Tracy for a minute, "I apologize for my direct nature, and cold delivery. As far as me being a Marine, no, I don't think so. Hmmm, while we're on the topic, I fucked a Marine one time, actually a Drill Sergeant. He said he wished he could drill me all the time. Damn, I get horny just thinking about his ass. Something about that damn uniform."

Tracy could not help but laugh at Meisha, "You are crazy as hell".

Meisha replied, "Yeah, I know, at least I got you laughing."

"You always do." said Tracy.

"And yeah, I heard she was a hoe but she never seemed that way to me. She was so friendly and down to earth at our first meeting, we clicked. I loved the way she seemed to care about her students. It was like we had known each other for a long time. I appreciated her concern for Jr., especially since he was placed in her class during the middle of the semester. Jr. was very fond of her, and you know he's very leery of people."

Meisha spoke in a serious tone, "Hey, not trying to be nasty, but obviously little Ms. Hoe worked some magic on your son also. Damn, an undercover hoe teaching children, what is the world coming to? You send your kids to school to get educated and the teacher is there to see whose father she wants to fuck, damn!" Meisha moved around to get more comfortable on the plastic covered sofa and asked, "Why in the hell have you chosen to cover your furniture with plastic? This is some 70's shit here."

Tracy looked her in the eye and with a nasty frown said, "Because they fucked on my chairs, all over my chairs. You will see, just wait until you see the tape. Then you will understand the 70's shit. "

"You honestly had no idea she was looking at your man?" asked Meisha.

"Honestly, no. I mean now that I think back to the start of her coming to visit, there were some things that I should have paid more attention to." said Tracy. "Maybe if they would have started fucking, I would have picked up on it. "

"Don't be a smart ass Tracy, I was just asking." said Meisha

Ignoring Meisha's comments, she continues to speak, "One day she came over and we were laughing and talking. Jamal had come in from the garage; shirtless and sweaty. His Levis were hanging, showing off his abs. I thought it was strange that her conversation suddenly shifted toward Jamal. She was smiling at him, which I just shrugged off as her being friendly. I thought how nice it was to have another friend that my husband likes. You know how some husbands can't stand their wives' girlfriends? I had heard she was a hoe, and should have listened."

Shaking her head left to right, Meisha said, "Well don't beat yourself up about it now. It's done. You are just too damn friendly and trusting. I've told you that a million times."

This time Tracy agreed with her, "You are so right. I am too damn trusting, but know one thing for sure is this bullshit has taught me a lesson. So, let me brief you a little more before I play the tape for you, here goes. That week on a Wednesday, my mom called and asked if there was any way I could come to D.C. for a visit that weekend. It was very unlike her to ask on such short notice, so I said yes, I would be there on Friday. I called my husband and explained to him what was going on. He said he could call his mom to come over and help with Jr., if he needed to. Well, when I got off the phone a thought hit me; his mom may be too busy running her business. "Wait!" Let me finish Meisha. I thought about Candy. That's the teacher. I only asked her if she could check with Jamal during the week to see if he needed help with Jr., because Jamal had been working long hours out at the farm. Candy had been so helpful with Jr., so I figured why not ask her. "

Meisha jumped right in, "Let me get this straight. You asked her to check in on your husband and son." Meisha held up her hand, "wait" let me finish, it's my turn now. You called this woman and let me guess; she said sure, no problem. Damn, Tracy if I didn't know you, I would think you done fell and bumped your damn head. Maybe I should check your head for bumps. Damn!"

"Very funny Meisha and you are right those were her exact words. NO PROBLEM. How could I have been so stupid?" Tracy sat there crying like a baby which made Meisha hurt for her friend.

"First right thing you've said today. How could you be so stupid? I'm sorry, please Tracy, stop crying. You weren't stupid. You were just too trusting with that bitch. Believe it or not, this shit ain't the end of the world. You got to get yourself together and figure out what's next. Now that we know she did what you asked and a little more, can I see this damn video you got? What luck those two had? How many people get caught fucking by a home security camera? I have to get this same set up with the cameras if I ever get married. Although, I don't think marriage is worth all this pain. Talk about evidence for the court, damn. You forgot to tell him to turn off the cameras and his dumb ass never thought to check. Didn't you say it even emails activity to you when it's activated?" Meisha didn't know whether to cry for Tracy or cry for Jamal's dumb ass because shit was about to hit the ceiling!

"That's right; it emails the video to both our email accounts. We had it installed when the news kept reporting so many break-ins last year." Tracy said.

Meisha said, "Good thing because had you not got it, who knows how long this affair would have gone on, right here in your personal space, your home. Damn."

Now with the tears under control, Tracy said, "that school must be hiring teachers with majors in education and minors in hoeing."

Meisha laughed, "Girl that sounds about right. But guess what? You gonna be alright. Meisha gonna help you get your life back in order."

"I will be informing the school board about Ms. Candy Bailey's behavior" said Tracy.

"Then you have to decide what to do about that lying, cheating ass Jamal." Meisha said. I wouldn't be surprised if he ain't been cheating the whole time. Of course that's just my opinion."

"Well Meisha, you know what they say, opinions are like assholes, everybody got one." said Tracy. They both fell out laughing together this time. Now, let's look at my lying, cheating ass husband's flick!" As Tracy picked up the remote control, Meisha said, "First let's pour a drink. I don't know about you but I need one. This is some off the chain shit going on. Make mine crown on the rocks, second thought, two shots, no ice."

Laughing, Tracy said, "Girl, you crazy as hell."

"That's what they say," Meisha continued to laugh.

So after both had drinks in their hand, Tracy pressed play and that's when it all came out that day. There was camera footage at the front door and from the interior, showing the open floor plan downstairs. It was all on tape and Jamal's dumb ass had no idea.

■■■

THE VIDEO TAPE

Who said hoes only come out at night?

She's no vampire,

Like you she walks day and night.

Always smiling; teeth so white.

Talking and laughing, seeing your man in her sight.

Sins of the Flesh

She has neither conscience nor friends,

Her desire and goal is to conquer men.

She prefers the faithful, playas won't do.

Hold on to your man or she'll do it for you.

****

Tracy left for her parent's home in D.C. on Friday evening, after having gone over everything with her husband. She had left earlier than planned because she didn't want to miss her hair appointment. -She kissed them both and told them she should be back in a week or less. Had she cancelled her appointment just this once, she might have seen Ms. Candy Bailey riding slowly through the neighborhood a few different times.

On Saturday morning, at 9:30 am, Mrs. Johnson, Jr's friends mom, arrived to pick up Jr. Jamal could see Jr's face full of excitement as he left with his friend and Mrs. Johnson. Jamal in sweats and a tee shirt waved bye and shut the door. He walked into the living room and stared at Tracy's picture, leaned over it and kissed it. He was missing Tracy. He wasn't used to her being gone without him. Now that JR was gone, the house was too quiet. He decided he would shower and head out to the farm to check on things. That was one of his occupations, the other was construction. He and Tracy owned their company and it was growing in size. The farm was his baby; he was born and raised in the country. You could take the man out of the country, but not the country out of the man.

He then headed toward the stairs to take a shower. He had hope that taking a cold shower would help with this hard dick situation. As he showered he thought about his wife. He was missing her terribly, but it wasn't just because of her being gone. Their sex life had really fallen off the charts, because of his long hours at work and Tracy being consumed with her hairdos. He had started leaving work earlier and putting someone else in second command at the farm, but Tracy seemed to always have an excuse lately. If it wasn't a headache, it was that damn hair.

The shower felt good but it was of no help relieving his need for a woman, preferably his wife. He didn't like going to sleep and not having Tracy in bed next to him. There had been mornings when he woke up with a smile. It wasn't because it was a new day; no it was a brand new day when he awoke to his wife slobbering on his dick. He had friends that bragged about their affairs on the side, women doing what their wives wouldn't do. He didn't have that problem with Tracy; she was his wife and his freak. But as of lately, his freak no longer existed. He thought about calling and asking her to please come home so he could tell her how much he needed her to be his wife in more ways than one. But he didn't want to be selfish or impatient with his wife.

He loved her deeply. He lusted and daydreamed at times about other women, but that was normal. He was human after all Jamal, his wife and son attended church most Sundays. Sometimes, they would stay in and watch the service on TV and relax. Jamal was trying to stay on the right path, but Tracy wasn't making it easy for him. One thing Jamal had learned was that, the spirit is strong but the flesh is weak. For this reason, he chose to go to work and stay close to home. He admitted that he believed he came out of the womb craving pussy. He had been a true player back in the day.

That all changed when he met and fell in love with his beautiful wife. Tracy was intelligent, caring and patient with him and their son. She was built like a brick house and kept her body tight since the first day he met her. She never complained about how much he worked and helped out whenever she was needed. Yes sir, Tracy had been all that he needed. He needed her to be that now. They were going to talk when she returned from her parents. Jacking off was not what a man should do if he had a wife. Just as he was showering, the doorbell rang.

It was Candy Bailey, standing there with her short coat and red stilettoes. Jamal could hear that lame ass ring of the doorbell, but wasn't quite finished with his shower. He stepped out of the shower, grabbed a towel and ran to the steps. As he ran to the top of the steps he yelled, "I'm coming, give me a minute." He couldn't hear a reply and went back into the bathroom, dried off and put on his robe and slid his bare feet into his slippers. Whoever it was, it better be damn important this early on a Saturday.

At the door, Candy smiled and yelled, "No problem. It's just me, Ms. Bailey."

There was no response but that was okay with her. She had more than enough time to wait with Tracy being miles away. She stood there horny, but patient. She was willing to wait as long as she needed to. She stood there remembering the first time she came to visit and Jamal walked into the house wearing only Levis, chest smooth like a baby's ass with sweat running down his six pack. What really got her attention was that trail of black hair starting below his navel giving directions to his man downstairs.

She had sized him up real fast. He was about 6'4 around 180lbs built like a true country boy, thick arms as if he had been cutting wood for a living. Upon staring at him, she felt her pussy warm up and later that day she realized she would have to wear a panty liner if she would be around him. Her pussy had leaked juices that were a product of seeing that man. She knew then, it was a must have. Her craving for this faithful man had kicked in. He was also attractive to her because he wasn't hanging out in the streets. Now she knew he was clean and not being shared. He was a family man and like other family men, they wanted to believe their wives were all they needed. At least that's what they told their wives. Wives were of no concern to her. It was all about her, a challenge, a good fuck and no commitments. She didn't want the husband, the kids or any other headaches that came with marriage. So yes, she would stand here at the door and wait. There was no rush at all. Her pussy was doing a countdown, wanting to cum.

Jamal dressed with only a robe and slippers walked downstairs to the door. He called out, "who is it?" Just as he got to the door and looked out the peep hole, he could see her.

"It's Candy, I mean Ms. Bailey, just stopping by to checking on you and Jr," she yelled. She was finishing the sentence when he opened the door. Once he saw her standing there, he was speechless. There she stood about 5'11, caramel skin, light brown eyes, no more than one hundred forty lbs. belonging to her breast and ass alone. She had on what appeared to be a short coat with the top buttons undone showing a thin tee-shirt of some sort.

"I hope I'm not here too early. Tracy asked me to stop and check on you guys if I had time." She said with a sexy smile.

He could feel his manhood growing harder when he glanced down at her long legs being held up by the red stilettoes. *Damn, damn, damn,* he thought to himself. He cleared his throat and said, "No, no it's not too early. Actually it's just me, JR left with a friend earlier. He is going to King's Dominion for the day and then he is having a sleepover at his friend's house. *Too much information told,* he thought to himself again. Jamal stepped to the side and said, "I'm sorry, come on in. I forgot my manners there for a minute. He could smell the Cashmere Mist on her. He knew what it was because he had bought his wife the same thing. It was sexy as hell. He watched her sashay pass him. Those legs seemed to get more and more attractive. He shut the door and as he did, she was making her way to the sofa. He didn't recall telling her to take a seat or asking her to. She needs to leave; he thought to himself, he was already walking around with a dick that felt like he was carrying a brick under his robe. It was really starting to hurt.

She sat down and asked him, "So how are you? Tracy mentioned that you weren't used to her leaving you and Jr alone."

He could have sworn she had a sneaky smile on her face. He told her, "We are okay. We are missing Tracy, other than that we making it. Now ask me that question in a few days and I don't know what I will say. She's only been gone one night. You knew that right?"

With a laugh, she said, "oh yeah, she did say she was leaving on Friday. I'm sure you both will be okay. I just thought I would check on you since I promised Tracy I would. I just happened to be in the area because I'm on my way to Victoria's Secret to pick up a few things."

There she was, sitting on their sofa looking sexy. What the fuck was a man to do? Damn! Victoria's Secret my ass he thought. She was there trying to turn a brother on. Done! Turned the fuck on! If he got turned on anymore, his belt on the robe would burst. He wanted to reach down and press his dick down, but he knew he couldn't do that.

"I'm sure Tracy appreciates knowing she has someone to check on us. Excuse the robe; I was just getting out of the shower." He decided to turn toward the stairs. "Before I go up to change, can I offer you a drink or something?" He realized he asked the wrong question, her eyes seem to look right below his belt. Then she looked up at him, her eyes showing a hint of what she wanted.

She said, "No, no I'm fine but thanks."

Fine she was...no lies there; fine as a matured bottle of red wine. Then he said, "well if you don't mind waiting a minute, I'm gonna run upstairs and throw some clothes on." He started toward the stairs. He turned around as she started to speak, "well, actually I would like to speak with you about something before you go upstairs."

He sensed what was going on. He thought to himself, "please not today, this chick wants to fuck. What's a brother to do when a hoe comes knocking at his door? Why did Tracy do this to him? Oh, so now it's Tracy's fault that this hoe is turning him on. He might be married, but he damn sure wasn't crazy. He turned around to see her undoing her coat. As she spoke he noticed there was no thin tee-shirt, it was a sheer dress that she was wearing. She wasn't planning on going to no damn store.

He could feel himself losing to his flesh. Hell, who was he fooling, his flesh had won when he opened the door and saw her. He walked toward her as if he couldn't hear her from the stairs. He was sure the secret was out now, sure she could see how his dick was swollen against the robe and pressing outward. He couldn't believe as he glanced down at her dress that she was completely nude underneath.

He cleared his throat once again, "ah, you said you need to speak to me before I go up to change?"

She peeped his hardness before he walked to the stairs, feeling her pussy juices stirring. She knew by his eyes that he could see her nipples pointing toward him. She stood directly in front of him.

"Jamal, can I ask you a question?" she said in a sexy tone.

"Sure, what is it?" he asked wishing his dick would get shy and play Houdini and disappear.

In almost a whisper, holding direct eye contact she asked, "Can you keep a secret?"

He knew he was in trouble now, stuttering he said, "Sssssure whhhhhat's wrong?"

"Well, to be honest Jamal, I wouldn't exactly say something is wrong, it's just not very right either. See, I want you." She gently opened his robe while he just stood there like he was shell shocked. She placed both hands around him and started to massage it. There he stood like a child, whispering, "Sure, I can keep a secret."

This fool had totally given up on trying to be strong. He was speechless and feeling helpless, almost wanting to call the police or some damn body to get this hoe out of his house. Hell, he needed saving and wasn't too proud to admit it to himself. He moaned out like a child that had been caught stealing candy, *but I can't, I am married*. But he never backed away from her. He stood there, like a soldier ready to take on the enemy by any means. Except there was only two ways to deal with this enemy, walk away or fuck her. To himself, he said, *I take the last choice for 500*. He knew it was over, the flesh had really won. To answer his question, "what to do when a hoe comes knocking? Fuck her, fuck her! What else could he possibly do in this horny weak ass state? Pussy he thought will bring a man down every time. Somebody ought to take pussy, put it in a box, put a chain around it and send it to the bottom of the sea. Then again, hell no, it's the main necessity for a man's wellbeing. Damn, damn, damn. As she stood there close to him, he grabbed her face, placed his mouth to her mouth, and as they both opened their mouths, he started sucking on her tongue like it was pure sugar in his mouth. He removed his hands from her face while still kissing her. He touched her thighs; they were smooth as he ran his hand up to her pussy. She had no panties on. As he reached her hole, he sighed. He could not believe how sweet she was to his touch. As he placed a finger in her honey hole, he could feel her juices.

He had been right, she came here to be fucked and who was he to send her away disappointed? He stopped for a second and led her over to the sofa she had sat on earlier. As he was leading her to lie down she stopped him. He thought she had changed her mind, but no, she had something else in mind. She opened his robe and removed it for him and changed standing positions and asked him to be seated.

"You sit down, this is all about you. I've got something for you," she said. As he sat down, he could still smell her perfume. She stood there and removed her thin dress to reveal nudeness. He was amazed at how beautiful her body was. The caramel tone was even all over, neither a scar nor scratch on it. Her breasts were firm and upright, nipples pointing out. Her pussy area was shaved bald, and beautiful, unlike other pussies he'd seen in the past. Some pussies seemed to look as if they had been rode hard and beat the hell up. Hers was so pretty, he wanted to taste her. It was so wet and he wanted to wet his throat with her juices. After her dress had been thrown to the side, she bent down on both knees, licked the top of his dick repeatedly and took him in her wet mouth gently. She was up and down on his dick like oil drill pumping for barrels of oil. He felt like he had to be the luckiest man alive. After a few strokes she squeezed her jaws a little more. Deep throating was her thing. She took about 8 inches into her mouth with a few inches remaining. She knew if she took it all in that he would come too quickly. He fell back on the sofa moaning. He didn't know if his dick would last much longer and he felt so helpless that something told him to stop her.

She was driving him crazy; he never had been sucked this way. This was dangerous, he even thought about hitting her in her head, but then came his release. He came like he never did before, not even in his playa years. He watched her, expecting her to get up, he reached for her, but she whispered, "no, not yet." She started at the bottom of his dick looking directly in his eyes, licking his entire nut right up to the head and swallowed. He thought to himself, "damn, damn, damn." Never had he felt like this. He needed her.

She didn't wait for him to make a move; she stood up and sat on the chair across from him. She stared directly into his eyes and challenged him to keep to his side of the room. When he saw her sit back on the chair and separate those long legs of hers, he got up to go to her.

She held up her hand and said, "No, stay where you are."

He could feel himself getting hard again and said, "What? I want you."

She said, "There's plenty of time for that, now I want to play a game."

He was almost sounding as if he was begging, "What? A damn game? What type of game?"

"It's a game that's gonna make this pussy better for you. Trust me. I call it the ABC'S." she replied.

"What are you talking about, the ABC'S?" he asked, watching her put her finger into her hole.

"I want you to watch me and say your ABC's slowly, very slowly and when you get to "Z" you can come over here and do as you please."

"Damn, girl you gonna drive me crazy." he said.

"That's the point," she said smiling and full of cum.

She started rubbing her clit and he started saying his ABC's. He was trying to go slow and while saying them, he was moving closer to her. He was on S and he could see the juices running out of her pussy, he thought he would never get to Z and she was clearly excited. He was on Z when he reached her, she knew what he wanted. He grabbed her hands with pure determination and placed them on her knees. He was gonna finish this job. He took his finger and ran it from her clit to her hole, inserted the finger once, twice and then a third time. This time he sucked his finger and smiled at her. She was about to burst, this game was turning her on. He then, spread her legs more and bent his head down and started to tongue kiss her pussy. His tongue was twisting and turning causing her muscles to tighten. She wanted to cum and had underestimated this man. Just as she yelled she was about to cum, he stood up and turned her over and grabbed hold of her ass and plunged his dick within the depths of her with no feelings of regret. He smacked her ass twice, while she started to shake, and said, "Damn." He fell back away from her body as she had yelled, "yes!"

They both were speechless, after a few minutes the guilt started to show on his face. After such an act of lust, she would have never thought she would turn around and see such disgust on his face. He looked at her as if he'd had a bad dream. Without saying anything, he jumped up and put on his robe and tied his belt has if he had to lock his dick up. She was standing now watching him, clearly not prepared for his reaction. He grabbed her clothes and jacket and held them out to her.

"Take it, get dressed and get out." He said angrily.

With an attitude, she said, "What? You made love to me and just like that you throw me out?"

He stepped to her and pointed his finger in her face, and said, "Did you just say we made love? Are you fucking crazy? This was a big fucking mistake. Put on your jacket and get the hell out of here. Don't you ever mention this to anyone and never come here again. Do you understand?"

She stepped back and put her jacket on, sliding her feet into her shoes, still not believing that he would react like this, "you can't be serious?"

He replied, "Oh, I'm more than serious. You planned this. You knew what you wanted and you came here with the intention of fucking." Walking to the door and placing his hand on the knob, he continued, "Now, get out!"

With her dress in hand, she stopped directly in front of him, so close that he could smell his nut on her breath. She whispered, "I came here and got what I wanted? Don't act like you didn't like it." With her free hand, she reached down and wiped her pussy and before he knew it, she had ran her hand across his lips, and said, "Oh yeah I got what I wanted and you liked the taste and the feel."

Before she could say anything else, he grabbed her hand, pushed her out the door and slammed it shut. He walked over to the sofa, sat down and yelled, "What have I done?"

Outside the door after almost falling from his push, she could hear him crying. She smiled and walked away feeling the power of control. She thought to herself, this wasn't over. He wasn't crying when she was on her knees, so don't cry now. She wanted him again and would have him until she called it quits. Tracy would never have to know.

Tracy and Meisha

Meisha jumped up and yelled, "Damn! That bitch! "

Tracy sat there crying all over again and turned off the video.

Meisha looks at her and said, "Hell no! They don't get to get away with this! What are you going to do?"

Trying to fight back tears Tracy said, "I don't know Meisha, I honestly don't know. I love him even after seeing this."

"What? Are you fucking crazy? After seeing this video? You know what; you just need time to think about it? But don't you dare let this break you down. Handle this shit Tracy! Make him feel the pain you are feeling."

"I know Meisha, I know. Something has to be done but I just don't know what, Tracy said, pouring another drink while crying.

CHAPTER 5
KARMA'S A BITCH

There are things being done in your neighborhood that you would be surprised to know about. There are individuals that choose to live out fantasies, and try different things to release their inner freak. I found after really giving it a lot of thought, I could not give Jamal another chance or my marriage. So I decided to leave, and rented a condo across town. It's been a year and I've started the process for obtaining a divorce. I have learned that it's not always about love. Happiness can just come from sharing desires with a stranger or just simply enjoying how someone makes you feel. I found a nice woman's group, a group where women shared secrets and engaged in affairs that would be smiled upon by many. No, not prostitution; just pure adult excitement. Not every woman's group is having bake sales, playing cards or having fundraisers. I can't help anyone else until I help myself. Call it selfish if you want. I call it getting mine!

There was a group that had been formed out in Prince George County, known as the RCRS (Roller Coaster Ride Seekers). Tracy was taken by surprise when she learned of this club. Basically it was a group of women looking for a night of ultimate sex with a stranger. She pondered on being invited to the hang with this group of women. She wasn't worried about competition among the women, just the meeting a stranger to sleep with was strange. She didn't have a problem being asked out on dates. Basically, at this point in her life she just needed a good fuck on a regular basis with no strings attached. Tracy decided to try something different. So she reached deep down inside and gathered the nerve to attend a meeting. She joined the club via her best friend, Meisha.

Meisha worked for the lady who created the club. She had never participated in the group other than attending meetings and listening. Since Meisha had returned from New York, all she seemed to have her mind was the man she had met there. But Meisha had mentioned that was just a fling and now she was in search of someone to help rid her mind of that man. Meisha had mentioned she had someone in mind but didn't think it was something she should pursue. Tracy told Meisha if she found someone interesting, she should try to get to know him.

So Tracy attended the first meeting with the group and had to admit it was unlike any other meeting she had ever attended. These women were professional women of different walks of life. All of them were looking for the same thing. The meeting was more of introductions and listening to others talk. Tracy met other women, who were first timers like herself. Once the meeting was over, Tracy had decided she would be back a second time. As far as taking a night with a stranger, she was still unsure. One thing she did know was that she needed to get laid and she didn't want to wait another year.

So Tracy went to her second meeting and after attending the second secret meeting, she started to feel less nervous. The idea of doing strangers was a little weird for her. That wasn't a normal thing for her. She had been with Jamal for so long; she had no desire to be with anyone else, especially a stranger. However, the meeting was quite interesting and enjoyable. With everyone out on the patio hanging out talking and holding drinks in hand, she stood taking in the breath taking view of where she was. Nancy Hamilton, the woman that created this club comes from a family of bankers, not the ones that sit at the drive thru window or the ones that sit in their cubicles hoping to get new customers. No, her family members were the owners of banks and lots of real estate.

This place was approximately thirty miles from the city, sitting on roughly five hundred acres of rolling green fields. As she stood on the patio, the view of the Olympic size pool was very attractive and inviting with a few lights to make it look romantic after the sun went down. Another female mentioned this was a getaway property and was available to all of the members whenever they needed it. Tracy could tell this was a tight knit group of women. It was a group of women looking for only sex. One thing about sex, it's universal. Everybody...whether black, white, or blue wanted sex. Nancy came out and asked everyone to come inside.

They entered what looked like a meeting room. It was large and immaculate yet inviting. Sofas were all put into a circular position and you could see flowers throughout the room. There was a bar in a corner that looked to have the same stock as your local ABC store. The women seemed to be right at home. They all took their seats with drinks in hand. Tracy was feeling really relaxed and anxious to get started. Tonight, she decided would be her first date.

"Ladies, ladies, could I please have your attention?" The tall slim white female was Nancy.

She looked to be in her thirties with long blonde hair, tall and very slim, but Meisha said she was forty-six. She looked like a Vogue model. Her voice was husky as if she was a smoker. However, I doubt that. Her skin was too perfect. She scanned the room as the attendees became quiet.

"Thank you! I can see that everyone seems to be enjoying themselves, please as usual help yourself to any of the hors d' oeuvres out on the patio. Welcome new members, I do hope you find pleasure in your new circles of friends. " She was smiling a happy but mischievous smile. "Let's get down to business." After all the introductions were made, they all sat and listened to the lady of the house speak.

"We have had a few applicants requesting to join our group, along with medical history reports. The plan for tonight is to choose our next date, for some their first date, in hopes of them finding excitement and maybe even a thrill. Who knows, you may even find yourself on a roller coaster ride!"

The room erupted into loud bursts of laughter.

"That's what I'm hoping for." A woman looking around and laughing said to the group. "A damn roller coaster ride."

"Then I'm hoping you get it." said Nancy in her husky voice, smiling.

"Before we go over our prospects for the evening, there's something I want to ask. Does anyone object to my brother coming in for a few minutes to tell you about a function one of our banks are having?" I noticed she said one of her banks. Must be nice living so large. Tracy considered herself comfortable but not rich. She was hoping to obtain a loan from the bank to buy Jamal out of their construction company. Everyone agreed and seemed to be over thrilled at the idea of seeing her brother. "Okay, I'll be right back," she said. They all began to talk and laugh once again.

Nancy appeared with a tall gentleman about 6'3" tan skin, beautiful Colgate smile, medium built. Nancy didn't look like her brother; his skin was darker than hers, a much deeper tan. I found out later, he was Italian and white. Nancy and her brothers had actually been adopted. Tracy thought to herself, whatever color he was, he was fine as hell. He walked alongside his sister with a strong confident aura about him.

"Here we are ladies, Max go ahead." Nancy sat down with us in the circle and he took a seat also.

He said his hellos and glanced around the room. For a minute, she thought he paused when he looked over at her. As the conversation went on about some fancy bank fundraiser, his glance seemed to fall on her several more times. She sat thinking to herself, what's his problem. She didn't think they had ever crossed paths, but maybe he thought he knew her from his bank. He said thanks for their time and started to leave. She could hear the women talking about attending the fundraiser. She sat sipping on her drink and talking. While sitting there, she suddenly remembered why he was looking at her.

He was the man she'd bumped into at the bank. She thought, *Bank! Wait a minute, he's the owner. That's it! Oh dear, he remembers me. Did he hear me practically beg for a loan? Was he looking at me as if I was a poor person looking for a handout? Oh, damn! Just what I need, I come here for something different and fun. I get Nancy's brother of all people staring at me. He probably was thinking how pitiful. She has no money and no man.*

Damn. She got up and walked to the bar and asked for another drink. This time it was whiskey straight, no rocks.

Nancy came back into the room; Tracy sat down drinking as if she hadn't had liquid touch her throat in years. Just as Nancy was about to start talking, Max was at the door motioning for her to come back out into the hall. She looked at him as if he was disturbing her. Once again, Nancy excused herself.

"What's up Max?"

"I want in!" Max said with a serious expression.

"What are you talking about? You want in on what?"

"On your group thing here."

"Oh! No way! This ain't your type of club," Nancy said shaking her head.

"Seriously Nancy I want in and immediately. You told me all about this and I want to join."

"Are you serious Max? You have said more than once, you can't believe I have such a group. You said how pitiful, a bunch of lonely women without a personal life. What's changed your mind?"

He turned and looked into the room. Nancy could tell immediately his eyes were fixed on the dark skinned lady laughing across the room. "You know her?"

"No, I don't know her but I want in!"

"She's new to the group and I am not sure if she'll take part tonight. Besides, isn't this your night to chill out at your cabin? What the hell is wrong with you? Are you running a fever? Besides, you are five years her senior. No harm brother, but these ladies are looking for a roller coaster ride."

"What? What the hell are you talking about sis?"

"Please Max, I don't have time for this, I gotta get back in."

Nancy turned to go and Max pulled her back.

"Nancy I am not kidding, I want in! I want her! I got an idea of what you mean a roller coaster ride. I won't only give that sweet smiling, sexy one a roller coaster ride, I'll take her to the park and. well …never mind", he said waving his hand. "Just get me in damnit!"

Nancy touched his hand and said, "Max go to your cabin, I will see what I can do. Damn, I can't believe my brother wants to have some fun." Max walked away with a smile and Nancy went back in the room of ladies, wondering what had just happened here."

"Hello ladies, so sorry, let's get down to the fun. First I would like to say out loud our goal especially so our new comers know what we are about." She looked around the room as the smiles got larger. She noticed that the girl Max wanted was indeed beautiful. She remembered at the first meeting, she wondered why someone as beautiful as she was single. But Nancy also remembered looks had nothing to do with finding good sex without strings being attached. She was still puzzled about her brother's interest in Tracy. Nancy continued speaking, "Our goal is to always remember what we want. What is that ladies?"

Suddenly all raised their glasses and yelled, "A roller coaster ride!"

'Exactly!" said Nancy and in a serious husky tone she started to speak. "A woman won't always be right. She won't always be wrong. She wishes to do right, yet yearns to do wrong. Doing wrong sexually is a high, a rush, a feeling of excitement, foreplay is the flirting, seeing how much he desires her, it's going up a roller coaster, stomach turning, breasts aching, vagina throbbing, gravity spreading her legs. Orgasm which is the ultimate goal is coming down off the ride with a strong sensuous breathtaking release along with all organs working twice as hard, long enough to make her feel faint." Nancy looked out at them and smiled.

"Is that not what we are looking for? Is that not what we want?" Nancy spoke like a politician, hoping for an agreement on this very important issue at hand.

They spent most of the evening talking and laughing and Nancy proceeded to read off the requests sent in from the male group. She also asked for requests. Each lady seemed to be excited and as she decided on her date, they picked up instructions and said good night and left. Some of them were still sitting there and suddenly Nancy walked over to Tracy.

"Hey Tracy, how are you enjoying things so far?"

"Oh great, everyone is nice and so full of excitement."

"Are you ready to try a date?"

"I am, but didn't know exactly who to choose from the list."

"I understand, I have a new comer to the male group and he wants very much to see you tonight. I can assure you he is a great guy and won't ask you of anything that you are not comfortable with. What you think?"

Tracy stood their excited and nervous. "Where would I meet him and how will I know who he is?" "Easy, take this paper; it gives the address of the cabin. Actually it's across the property and it's the largest cabin on the property. He's hoping that you will come."

Tracy smiled and took the paper. She looked at Nancy and smiled, "Wish me luck!"

"You'll be okay. I do hope you find your roller coaster ride." Nancy mischievously said.

"Me too," Tracy said as she left.

Nancy sat down after all of her guests left and waited for her lover of five years to arrive. She could not help wondering how things would go with Max and Tracy. But they were two willing adults and it was none of her business. She texted her brother, that Tracy was on her way. She also told him, she was beginning to think he was sick. He texted back, "LOL".

Max thought about this sudden desire for this strange woman. What was it that had drawn him to her? Here he was sitting in this cabin, not just horny but full of desire for this stranger. He was not even sure how to start this evening out when she arrived. He was no stranger to sex, but something was different about this. He was excited and aroused after reading his sister's text. He rubbed his dick and whispered, "Almost time, just a little more patience."

He had decided that since this was their first night, he'd make sure she would feel damn good. This was the woman whom he had bumped into at his bank. He could still smell that sexy Euphoria on her skin. He didn't know at the time the name of the perfume, but he had been so consumed with thoughts of her, he decided to have a few expensive perfumes delivered to him. Euphoria was the name that this mysterious woman wore so sexually. This was not going to be just a roller coaster ride.

It would not be a roller coaster ride for that she would actually act out. He had something better planned. He was determined to start with something that would have her choosing him to spend her next night with. He had Lydia, the house keeper; bring over a new curtain for the shower. Lydia couldn't understand why. She had said to him that everything in his master bath had been replaced two weeks ago. He covered by saying the curtain was for a friend of his who was in need of a new look for his bathroom. He watched the clock, it was almost time.

He ran down the hall to the kitchen, removed the vase of flowers from the large oak table that sat six people and proceeded to cover it with the curtain. The candles he needed were in the kitchen. The candles had been there for months, he had hope that a day like this would come. However, he realized that he didn't think it would be this urgent for him. He could not get the image of her in his bank out of his mind. He dreamt about this woman.

His guy at the bank asked him how he knew this woman. He had told him that wasn't important. But the guy tried to get an answer, because it was so odd for the bank owner to step in and change the decision of a loan manager to accommodate a stranger. He knew it was an odd thing to do, but it was his bank after all. He just needed to be with this woman. He wasn't sure if this was just a desire for sex or something else.

As Tracy drove across the property looking for the cabin, she realized she was not only feeling good from the drinks but was horny as hell. She was tired of masturbating. Once in a while was okay but a couple times a day was starting to worry her. Besides, she was sure the manicurist wondered why there was always that one short nail. Oh well, she probably knew. She thought everyone has tried to please themself at some point in their life. She was a little nervous, but calm when she reminded herself of the situation at hand. It's just a night of looking for fun and of course a roller coaster ride. It wasn't like she was looking for a husband. Smiling, she spotted the cabin or least what they called a cabin. It was indeed larger than the others. It had a front porch that seemed to wrap about the cabin, along with glass doors.

Flowers along the porch and out over on the grass looked like a small bear lounging. When she stopped the car its head popped up. Wow! No bear but what a huge dog. Mastiff, she assumed and later found out she was correct. Here I go, she thought to herself, looking in the mirror to verify she was still looking good

Stepping out onto the porch comes a tall man with a white tee and jeans with a few holes in them. Whoever he was, he was sexy as hell in those raggedy jeans and barefoot. What? Looking closer, she could not believe her eyes. It was Nancy's brother. Talking about someone comfortably at home, he surely was. He smiled a gorgeous smile and yelled, hello. Her pussy meter went from a five to a ten in seconds.

"Don't mind the dog. He's an oversize baby. Trust me." He walked down to meet her."

"Hi." She said. "Do I have the right cabin?" She seemed to get nervous.

"You can get out, I promise he won't hurt you. " Just as she got out of the car, he was sure he had made the right decision. She was absolutely beautiful. Tall, slim, with dark skin that looked smooth as butter, and Those gorgeous eyes. He could picture his tanned dick lying against her dark skin. Just as he was the first time he saw her, he felt himself turned on all over again. Her eyes were a light brown, sexy as hell. What an odd yet beautiful combination. Her haircut was a natural cut close to her head. The small shorts and low cut top showed her sexiness. He could see how appealing her brightly painted toes were in her open toe sandals. She was definitely dressed for a comfortable evening. After all, he remembered his sister saying this was no fancy affluent club.

He had to get his thoughts together, she was speaking. "Yes you do." Reaching out with gentleness about him, he took her hand in his and walked her up the steps into the cabin. It had a fresh smell, another place immaculately decorated. It's a man's home, not too much furniture but enough to be comfortable. He reached out for her bag. "I'll take that and place it on the sofa for you, if that's okay."

"Sure." It was an instant attraction. He walked close to her and for some reason, she was no longer nervous. He leaned in and gave her a small kiss. That's when sparks seem to start.

"I was told that this is a first time for both of us."

"Yeah." She said with a small smile, she really thought having two drinks would ease her nerves, but she decided she needed more to help her relax. "How do we ugh start?"

He gathered her hand and with the other, turned the volume of music up just a little. John Legend's, "Tonight" started play. Suddenly out of nowhere, he pulled her to him and started to kiss her on her lips and greedily he went down to her breast. This man was acting hungry as hell and at the same time turning her hell on.

He seemed to be nibbling on her nipples with her shirt still on. At the same time, he began to undo her shirt. He took a break and looked up.

"Please tell me if I am moving too fast, it's just that I was turned on the moment I saw you."

'No, no, it's okay," she said barely able to talk with him nibbling on her breast.

She assumed he was talking about seeing her tonight at the meeting. She was hoping that he knew what he was doing because her panties were definitely starting to get wet. As she thought that, he ran his hand down her stomach slowing until he reached her private. He rubbed her vagina with her pants still on all while continuing to feed on her breasts. He stopped and looked directly at her eyes feeling like she was putting him under some kind of spell, and said while reaching to undo her blouse,

"Can I, may I please remove your blouse? You are so beautiful. "

She was thinking to herself, *did he just ask for permission? Hells yeah, take the damn blouse off.*

Still shocked and turned on she said, "Okay. Sure."

Glad she said yes, because now he had a breast in each hand and took turns with each one, he was sucking as if he expected milk to come out, she reached down and held her own breasts and watched him. She felt like she was breast feeding a grown ass man. This really got her pussy into an uproar. He suddenly stopped and was breathing rather hard. It was hard for him to stop but he didn't want to scare her off. This was the woman he had seen at his bank. He was intrigued and turned on at the first sight of her. He had overheard her speaking to one of loan officers. Her voice got his attention first, and when he looked up to see her, his manhood immediately became hard.

He was surprised at himself and could not get her off his mind for days. He had actually planned to schedule a meeting with her the next time she had business there. He asked her if she would like a glass of wine and she said yes. He reached for her hand and led her to the kitchen. Once they got into the kitchen, he smiled at her while reaching for the glasses. She stood there looking sexy as hell and he could feel his dick starting to swell once again.

He put the glass on the counter, poured the drinks and walked toward her. What was it about this woman that he could not control himself? She could see that he wanted her and she felt the same way. She couldn't help but notice the table which appeared to have a shower curtain for the cover. She knew he had enough money for a table cloth. But she pushed that out her mind, and took a sip of her wine. He stood there and watched her for a minute. Once she had placed her glass down, he did the same thing. He kissed her lightly on the lips and lifted his hands to rub her breasts again.

"I know I said wine, but let's do this first. Please!" he moaned.

"Okay, I see you're reading my mind." She said.

She had a sexy red bra with the snap in the front which made it easier for him to undo. He looked at her dark caramel breast with their dark nipples sticking out at him. He started to feed once again. He licked her stomach up and down and across it as it was sugar, her knees began to buckle. She was beyond turned on. She had to wonder only for a second had she underestimated what could happen with this stranger.

He looked at her and asked, "May I please give you something?"

She whispered almost speechless, "Yes."

He bent down and undid her shorts and slid them down slowly. He then picked her up around her waist and sat her in the center of the thick oak table. She wasn't sure what was going on, but she wasn't afraid. No fear from this man, only excitement. He moved over to the sofa and came back with a large pillow and gently place behind her back.

"This is for you to be comfortable and so that you won't slide too much." He said smiling.

"May I ask what this is about? The kitchen table and the pillow. I don't think the table can hold us both." She said.

"It doesn't need to hold us both. I won't be putting my full body weight on it. The table is for you, beautiful." He saw her eyes look at the shower curtain. "Ah! The shower curtain is to catch your juices. "

She was thinking he was into some freaky shit. But she still wasn't scared. She was more interested in relieving this cum buildup he had caused to stir within the depths of her pussy. He bent down in front of her and opened her legs wide. He didn't ask her to lay back; he knew she would do that on her own. He only had to get this thing started; the rest would take care of itself. She could feel him licking up and down her vagina, each time reaching her clit and sucking on it for a second or two. She thought she would explode any minute. He stopped and looked up at her with lips wet from the juices of her pussy.

It was only a second before he returned, he only wanted to see her eyes and just as she fell back and her body started to react, and her legs started to tremble from the pleasure he was giving her and He looked up and used his fingers to help her feel a slow release that lingered on in her vagina. He saw her eyes water and felt like he was in more than infatuation. Once she was done, he slid her backwards a little and started to lick the juices on her thighs and then he blew her mind. He bent down and licked the shower curtain and she could hear him slurp her liquids up and once he was done.

He picked her up and sat her on the marble counter, all she could say was, "fuck me".

"No, not yet, not yet love." He went back down again. She moaned while he continued teasing her clit.

So she went with it and there was that ride up the roller coaster, except there was no squeaking of rails, just her moans. His tongue was working some extreme magic. Her heart beat faster, breasts started to ache, and pussy wanted release. She wanted to be carried to the top of the coaster. Suddenly he stopped. Thinking to herself, *what the fuck?* He stood up and leaned toward her gently kissing her. He picked up a little off the counter and pulled her closer, so that they faced each other and her legs wrapped around his waist. She could feel his heart racing along with hers. His dick was hard as a piece of bark off an old oak tree. It was starting to pain so he leaned forward while holding onto her waist and plunged into her. It was wetter than he imagined it would be after she had cum once. As he pushed into her, she gave back to him and they came hard together. Each one moaning like animals in the wild. It felt to them both like the clouds opened up and a storm was released. Pure magic is what this was and neither understood it. Leaving their clothes behind on the kitchen floor, he carried her down the hall to his bedroom.

He reached the room and placed her on a large, lush king size bed. "This will be the first of the many great nights we have together."

She didn't really know what he meant but assumed it was horniness speaking. You know a man will say he's gonna jump off a bridge if he having sex. That's just the way it is. But the part of a great night, she didn't doubt him at all. He lay beside her, placing an arm around her. They lay like sleeping babies throughout the night, each one dreaming about this night all over again.

So Tracy awoke the next morning around 8 am, still exhausted from the previous evening. She hadn't drunk a lot last night, but it did seem like a dream. She turned over in the huge bed to find herself alone. Then as she looked up, she saw him. One side of the large bedroom was all glass with sliding doors. Outside of the doors, that tall, thick, tanned man sat at a patio table reading the paper. Right beside him laid his dog, Karma. She sat up and pulled the sheet over her naked body, thinking back to being carried to bed. Had she missed something here? She had been under the impression that they would fuck and she would leave. After all she was just after a wild roller coaster ride.

Walking toward the door with the sheet pressed to her body she thought how it was a wild ride but it seemed like something deeper had happened between the two. She could have sworn she heard thunder and rain last night. But she put it off to the two drinks she had. Just as she got to the door to open it, he looked up. Damn he sure was fine. The smile he gave her was like a beam of sunshine. Karma looked up in her direction also and tilted his head. She guessed he was trying to figure who she was and why was she still there.

She stepped out onto the patio returning his smile. "Uh, hello"

He stood up and started toward her, "Hello. I decided not to wake you. You looked like you were dreaming."

"Um, I'm not sure what to say. Thanks for the night maybe? This was my first time, I um…."

He touched her lips and said, "No explaining needed. This was my first time also."

She looked confused, "Your first time? I assumed since this was your sister's club, that you were a member."

"Oh, no. I just happened to come speak to the members on a night when you attend. By the way, you aren't really a stranger to me."

The previous night starting running through her head and she started wondering was he some kind of freak. "What do you mean you're not a stranger? Sorry, but have you confused me with someone?"

He stepped inside, closing the sliding door behind him. Karma raised his head, looking at his master and decided to go back to sleep.

He reached out for her hand and said, "Truth be told, I have seen you a few times at the bank. Every time, it seemed like you were there to torture me more and more. "

He touched her lips again to quiet her. "Please don't think I am crazy. It's just that you are a beautiful woman. I remember what you had on the last couple of times you came. Remember we bumped into each other? Well, that really did it. I could smell your sexy scent and it stayed with me for the longest time. Euphoria, I believe it is. Your perfume; correct?"

She laughed and was in awe, "Well I see you know your perfume. But you never said anything to me. May I ask why?"

"You had been with a man the first couple of times and I found out you were married. So I decided to mind my business. Then as luck would have it, I saw you last night. I wasn't about to miss the chance to see you or touch you."

"Oh, okay. I think I understand. Well, I'd better be going. Are my clothes still in the other room?"

"Do you have to leave right now? I mean is there a man at home or something you can't miss for a while?"

She laughed a little more saying, "No. there's no man or anything important. I just figured we were done." She started feeling her throat getting dry. She couldn't figure out what was going on. They barely knew it other.

He was really looking sexy and very tempting, but he couldn't possible want more time. Could he?

This time he stepped even closer and said, "Can I ask you something?"

"Sure. Anything. "she said.

He was touching her hair lightly with both hands. It took so much control for her to not just drop the sheet in front of her.

"Well, did you enjoy last night the way I did? I mean did you have your roller coaster ride?"

Embarrassed by the statement she said, "Yes. I had my roller coaster ride and more." She started giggling and asked, "Can I ask you a question?"

"Sure you can."

"What's your name? I mean, I heard your sister call you Max. Is that your real name?"

"Actually it's Maximillian, Max for short." He said as he stepped closer.

He liked her smile and laughter. He brought his hands down some, and held her face and gave her one hell of a kiss. She could feel the heat between her legs start to rise. She was thinking if she could handle this man eating her pussy out the way he had the previous night. She realized she wanted him to do it again. She decided the hell with going home to an empty apartment and missing out on this. One more time won't hurt.

Tracy asked if she could take a shower because she could see in his eyes what was coming next. She could feel herself being turned on by this Maximillian. He gave her a robe and told her where to find the bath cloths and towels. He then went to another room for his shower. He had only one request of her. He asked her to be nude and stretched across his bed when he returned. Tracy smiled and went into the bathroom.

After completing her shower, she did as he requested and lay comfortably on his bed. He returned in the nude himself. Tracy thought he was the sexiest man alive. He walked over to her, stopped and looked down at the sheet and started to remove it. She lay there, as he started to kiss her breast and then bent down and licked her stomach and stopped just before reaching the bottom. She was holding her breath. He stood up and smiled at her.

"Would you like a treat?" he asked mischievously

"Max, what kind of a treat? I don't usually eat this early in the morning."

He ran his large hands down her stomach and caressed her pussy and said, "Oh, you won't be eating. I have a treat for you."

She couldn't help but wonder what had she gotten herself. But she realized she felt comfortable with him for some reason.

"Sure Max, I'd like a treat." She said turned on. Her pussy started to throb the minute he touched it. It was the way he said treat that had her turned on even more. Max removed his hand and walked nakedly to the bedroom door.

Looking at her, he said, "I'll be right back, don't go anywhere beautiful."

Tracy started laughing and replied, "Well I can promise you, I won't be going anywhere like this."

Tracy could not believe how much she was enjoying this. This man had for one night removed all stress from her mind. Max walked into the kitchen and opened the fridge. Bending down as if he had lost something, he started moving things around.

"Ah, there you are." He said. He opened the container of peaches and tasted for freshness.

They were just right. He grabbed the container and removed a few to place in a bowl. Excited and horny, he put the container back in the fridge and shut it. He started back down the hall with his dick swelling while thinking of the pussy in his bed. He entered the bedroom with the bowl in his hand and his dick standing to attention. Tracy sat up and held the sheet covering her breast.

"Max, I told you I don't want food."

"Two things beautiful, number one, these peaches are for you. Well they are for you but I will only be eating them. Number two; please remove the sheet from your breasts." He said smiling.

When Max said something about eating, Tracy felt her pussy throbbing. So she happily dropped the sheet and smiled. At that moment he walked over to the bed and placed the bowl on the nightstand beside it. Max reached around and picked up two slices of peaches from the container and smiled at her. He gently ran the soft but cold peaches over her tender brown nipples and she shivered from coldness and the heat that was building inside her.

Tracy could not believe she was being served like this so early in the morning. She thought how Jamal never did this, but quickly erased him from her mind. Max made a trail with the fruit down her stomach past her navel. Tracy laid there closing her eyes, enjoying the wild feelings he was stirring inside her.

He didn't have to tell her to open her legs. She did that willingly. He had created a heat between her legs that needed to be released in the worst way. Once her legs were open, he moved around to the front of her and crawled toward her. Naturally Tracy brought her legs up, bending her knees as she had done the previous night on top of the table. He started rubbing the peaches up and down her inner thighs and finally he took one hand and opened her wet pussy lips exposing the pink flesh inside.

Max took the hand holding the peaches as juice had already ran down his finger, he slid them inside her. He dipped the peaches in the wetness a couple of times and looked up at her. He was putting the peaches in and out licking them as if the peaches were chips and her pussy juice was salsa. Then he started to eat the peaches.

Tracy was about to explode, her body was tensing up and legs started to tremble from the need of having him inside of her. Her mind was yelling, just fucking do it. It was like he was torturing her. He finally buried his head between her legs devouring her. He was sucking on her clit as if he was making love to it. Tracy started moving her butt around while her legs were trembling. He sensed she was about to cum and he wanted them to do it together. So he rose up and positioned himself above her, hungrily he started to tongue kiss her. Then he looked down at her nipples and started squeezing them as if he expected milk to appear. Slowly he lowered himself down on her. As soon as the head of his dick touched her pussy's entrance, she raised up.

He couldn't contain himself anymore and dived as deep as he could into her pussy. Watching her, they fucked hard and fast. She could feel every inch of him entering depths unknown inside her. They rode the roller coaster together becoming one. Neither realized it but the clouds had opened and raining was pounding on the roof. They moaned and yelled out together as both experience the wildest orgasm that either of them had ever experienced. They laid there one on top of the other exhausted.

Outside the window, he stood peeping in with tears running down his cheeks. He hurt because it was what he had done that ran her into a stranger's bed. Just as he turned to leave, he came face to face with the teeth of Karma. He thought the dog was dead lying on the deck. Karma let out the most vicious growl which alerted Max and Tracy. They ran to the door both nude and saw Jamal pressed up against the house with Karma daring him to move.

Jamal looked over at Tracy and she saw the tears. Tracy walked from the door as Max stepped out yelling for Karma to back down. Tracy returned to Max's bed feeling no regret.

Jamal left as Max asked him to before he called the police. Jamal became angry at himself while driving away. He was thinking how Karma was a bitch and why had he put that GPS on Tracy's car. He drove until he reached his destination. She was still there; he needed a good old fuck.

Stay tuned for more Sins of the Flesh!

Thank you for reading. Please don't forget to leave your review.

Sins of the Flesh

Sins of the Flesh

www.ingramcontent.com/pod-product-compliance
Lightning Source LLC
Chambersburg PA
CBHW071404170626
46811CB00003B/1252